JACKIE RAE

A SAN FRANCISCO STORY

KIP PEARSON

www.dizzyemupublishing.com

DIZZY EMU PUBLISHING
1714 N McCadden Place, Hollywood, Los Angeles 90028
www.dizzyemupublishing.com

Jackie Rae – A San Francisco Story
Kip Pearson

ISBN: 9781706958758

First published in the United States
in 2019 by Dizzy Emu Publishing

www.dizzyemupublishing.com

JACKIE RAE

A SAN FRANCISCO STORY

KIP PEARSON

JACKIE RAE. A SAN FRANCISCO STORY

Written by

Kip Pearson

July 17, 2019

1527 San Anselmo Ave
San Anselmo, CA 94960
415 686 4785
Kspcal@comcast.net

FADE IN

SAN FRANCISCO. 1973

Opening shot is of the Golden Gate Bridge. Fog is spilling
over Twin Peaks is followed by a rolling street scene of
older victorian houses with wide stoops. People in hippie
attire are wandering by.

EXT.CORTLAND STREET-DAY

A Harley roars up the street and backs into the curb in front
of Wild Side West, an old neighborhood lesbian bar. The
rider, JR, takes off her helmet to reveal a young woman in a
short mullet and denims. She is medium build with a very
athletic bearing and clearly on the butch end of the scale.
She lights a cigarette hanging from the side of her mouth and
swaggers in the bar.

INT.WILD SIDE WEST-DAY

JR joins CAT, another young dyke. FRANKIE, an older butch is
behind the bar. There are a couple of other women talking at
the other end of the bar and two others are playing pool.
All are dressed blue collar in flannel shirts and work boots.

                    FRANKIE
          JR! Aww the baby dykes are here.
          What'll you have, kids?

                    JR
              (Slapping Cat on the back)
          A draft for me and one for her.
          What's happenin, Cat?

                    CAT
          The guy at the union says they
          might have room for another girl,
          they gotta make a quota these days.

                    JR
          How is it?

                    CAT
          The guys are all jerks, harassing
          me in this way and that, like
          elbowing me into the doorway on
          purpose. The teacher had to remind
          them to be nice to the new
          people...'Even the girl', he says.
          And they all laugh.

                    JR
Maybe I should try and get in too,
actually learn a respectable skill.

                    FRANKIE
You know, baby, we gotta be twice
as good to get half the respect
those guys will get just for showin
up.

                    JR
My brother, Mark just got into
Harvard Law and everyone is sooo
proud of him. Especially Dad, who
can't wait to bring him into the
firm the minute he graduates.

                    CAT
Go back to school, JR, and find
some other way to kick some ass.
You already have a pretty good
ticket.

                    JR
Can't see myself lawyering like
everyone else in the family. I need
to be outside doing real work. I
have to go home for Grandma's
funeral in a couple days and face
all that.

                    CAT
Sorry to hear that. Were you close
to your grandma?

                    JR
Not at all! She pretty much hated
me. Not exactly the little princess
they were expecting me to be.

                    FRANKIE
So what happened to Grandma?

                    JR
She got hit by a cab.

Silence for a moment then they all start laughing.

                    CAT
Sorry to laugh but that's kinda
funny.

                    JR
It's ok, really.

                    CAT
          Families. Are they all going to
          call you Jackie Rae and expect to
          see you in makeup and a dress?

                    JR
          Please don't call me that. That is
          the old life I left behind when I
          moved to San Francisco.

                    CAT
          That's why we all came here, right
          Frankie?

                    FRANKIE
          True that! To San Francisco.

They toast by clinking their glasses and downing them in one
long swallow.

                    CAT
          Oh hey, Frankie, I came up with a
          name for our softball team. The
          Fringe.

                    FRANKIE
          I LIKE IT.

                    JR
          Right on.

INT.CHURCH-DAY

Organ music is playing as mourners file into the church. JR,
with a very masculine look in a dark boys suit jacket and
white shirt, is sitting alone a few rows back from the front.
Her hair is slicked back.

The family: DAD, MARK, and his fiancé, BARBARA, AUNT RAE and
a couple of older women file in to sit in the front. Dad is
very distinguished looking in an expensive suit, mid 50s,
trim and graying with a sophisticated bearing. He glances
over with a weak smile, the other family members look over at
JR with curiosity, some with obvious disapproval. Cousin
SURFER DAVE, early 20's, in a suit jacket, flip flops and
long hair sits a few seats away from her. He catches JR's
eye and they nod in solidarity.

EXT.GRAVESIDE-DAY

JR joins Dad, Mark and Aunt Rae in the first row of folding
chairs. Barbara and Surfer Dave are in the row behind them.

No one speaks. They face the camera in what could be a family portrait.

FREEZE FRAME. CAMERA SHUTTER CLICKS.

INT.UPSCALE SUBURBAN HOME-DAY

The mourners are mingling around the living room. Mark is slender and tan, dressed in a conservative designer suit, approaches JR. They stand side by side without facing each other.

                    MARK
               (clearly annoyed)
          Well look who decided to grace us
          with her presence. We weren't sure
          you would show.

                    JR
               (cooly avoiding his
                snarkiness)
          Why's that?

                    MARK
          You never showed her or Mom any
          respect when they were alive, why
          now?

                    JR
          Let it go, Mark. I hear you got
          into Harvard, good for you.

                    MARK
          Thank you. When are you going back
          to school?

                    JR
          I'm not sure if I will. I'm looking
          into the electricians union.

Mark turns to look directly at her with disdain.

                    MARK
               (back to being annoyed)
          The electricians union? That
          would've made Mom REAL proud. I
          always assumed you would be a cop
          or a marine the way you love to
          knock people down.

                           JR
                      (shrugging)
                Can't do the uniform thing.

                           MARK
                Well, good luck with all that, just
                piss away this family and all this
                opportunity. You know you could
                have dressed like a girl for just
                this once. Mom would have been
                horrified to see you show up
                looking like a guy.

Mark turns away shaking his head.

                           JR
                I can't do that uniform either. My
                regards to Barbie.

Surfer Dave approaches.

                           SURFER DAVE
                Hey there cuz. What's happenin?

                           JR
                I just got a scolding from Mark,
                the perfect son. Good to see you,
                man.

                           SURFER DAVE
                Yeah, I saw. Hey they don't much
                want to see me here either. Stank
                Eye Mark has hated me since we were
                kids. Remember when we used to
                race those lasers down at Alamitos
                Bay. You kicked everybody's butt.

                           JR
                Too bad the club wouldn't let me
                join the team, I probably could've
                helped them win a few times.

                           SURFER DAVE
                      (laughing)
                For sure. Then there was that time
                at the beach party when you knocked
                Roberto on his ass because you
                thought he was trying to feel that
                drunk girl up.

                           JR
                He WAS trying to feel up that girl!
                She was passed out!

                    SURFER DAVE
          You scared the crap outta him. He
          still calls you the girl avenger.
          It was funnier than shit.
          Hey...outside?

EXT.UPSCALE SUBURBAN HOME-DAY

JR and Surfer Dave exit the patio doors and step behind some
hedges out of view of other guests. He lights a joint, takes
a long draw and passes it over to JR, who accepts with a
smile. She takes a long draw herself. They quietly relish a
peaceful moment before coming back to reality.

                    JR
          Hey what are you up to these days?
          Still in school?

                    SURFER DAVE
          No way, man. I embarrassed them so
          bad with my grades that they let me
          quit. I lasted about a semester.
          Doin nothin but ridin the waves and
          gettin high. Tendin bar at the
          club, that's about it. You still up
          in Frisco?

                    JR
          Yeah. I love it there. It's like
          being in a whole new country. Just
          don't know what to do next, you
          know. I only know what I DON'T want
          to do.

                    SURFER DAVE
          I'm sure it's been real hard since
          that thing with your Mom.

JR acknowledges with a nod.

                    JR
               (with a sigh)
          Well, I guess it's time to give my
          regards to Dad and Aunt Rae.

                    SURFER DAVE
          How long are you gonna be around?
          Let's have breakfast at the Egg
          Heaven tomorrow and catch up.

                    JR
          Sure, man. 10?

                    SURFER DAVE
          Cool. I think I can get up that
          early.

Surfer Dave gives her an encouraging high five as she turns
to go back inside.

INT.UPSCALE SUBURBAN HOME-DAY

As JR approaches them, the relatives see her and turn away.
Aunt Rae is a serious, sophisticated upper middle class
matron with a very tight face.

                    JR
          Aunt Rae, sorry about Grandma.

                    AUNT RAE
             (avoiding eye contact)
          Well, thank you but you really
          didn't need to be here.

                    JR
          And why wouldn't I come?

Dad steps up to take her arm and guide her away toward the
bar. A couple of others mourners move to the side to make
room for them. The bartender is cleaning glasses.

                    DAD
             (almost whispering)
          Rae's a little sensitive right now
          but I'm glad you are here.

                    JR
          I thought it was important
          despite...everything.

                    DAD
          It's been kind of hard on your
          aunt, you know. She loves you even
          though she doesn't understand
          your... choices.

                    JR
             (annoyed)
          Yeah, my 'choices'. The one she and
          Mom tried to get me shock treatment
          for when I was 13.

                    DAD
          It didn't happen, did it?

                    JR
          Only because of you.

Awkward pause.

                    DAD
          Gin and Tonic?

                    JR
          Sure.

Dad signals to the bartender who sets the drinks up. Another
awkward pause as they sip their cocktails.

                    DAD
              (turning to her to draw
               her attention back)
          Mark just told me you aren't going
          back to school. Something about the
          electricians union?

                    JR
          It's honest work, Dad and it's
          important that women get into these
          kinds of jobs. Not everyone wants
          to stay home and be a housewife. I
          need to find something that suits
          who I am.

                    DAD
          You could go to law school and come
          work at the firm.

                    JR
          And marry some guy that wants to
          make partner and still be
          somebody's housewife? C'mon Dad,
          can you really see me doing that?
          Mergers and acquisitions really do
          not appeal to me.

                    DAD
          It's lucrative work and the firm is
          growing. We're landing some very
          big clients. Kiddo, as fearless and
          aggressive as you are, you would
          make a hell of trial lawyer, better
          than... well, your brother to be
          honest. There aren't many women in
          the field, you know, you could
          still be the pioneer.

                    JR
          Wouldn't I have to wear a dress?

                    DAD
                 (big sigh)
          We all have to make sacrifices.
          Just think about it, ok?

                    JR
          I have to do this on my own, Dad.

Dad gives her a warm encouraging smile and nods. They are
joined by a couple of other men who engage Dad. JR looks over
to see Aunt Rae staring at her and she sees the face of her
mother looking back with the same scowl on her face.

INT.SCHOOL HALLWAY-DAY FLASHBACK

JR's mother is furious as she drags 8 year old JR out of the
principal's office. JR is in denims, a t-shirt, baseball cap
and a cape. Another mother is comforting her crying son
outside the office.

                    MOM
          Suspended for 3 days for fighting!
          What is the matter with you?

                    JR
          He had it coming. He was teasing
          that Mexican girl.

                    MOM
          You bloodied his nose for god sake!

JR has a satisfied grin on her face as she is dragged along.

                    MOM (CONT'D)
          And take off that stupid cape!

INT.UPSCALE SUBURBAN HOME-DAY-FLASH FORWARD

JR's little kid grin fades as Aunt Rae's glare brings her
back to the present.

INT.EGG HEAVEN CAFE-DAY

JR and Surfer Dave are paying for their meal. The cafe hasn't
been updated for years. Several women are demonstrating with
signs and chanting on the sidewalk outside the front door.
The owner RALPH, the scruffy owner in his 50's, is handing
her change.

JR is in a tank top showing her muscular shoulders and jeans cut off above the knees. Surfer Dave is in a colorful tank top and board shorts.

                    JR
          Ralph, what's all this noise?

                    RALPH
          I guess they don't like my decor.

He points to a poster of a bikini clad woman standing next to a side of beef behind the counter and shrugs. JR and Surfer Dave step outside.

EXT.EGG HEAVEN CAFE-DAY

Surfer Dave notices JR watching the women protesters.

                    SURFER DAVE
          Hey we should team up some night
          and go chase girls.

                    JR
          Sorry, don't need a wing man and
          too bad you have to chase.

                    SURFER DAVE
                    (laughing)
          I'm sure you don't! Catch ya later.

                    JR
          Take care, man.

JR stops to watch the protesters with signs that read EGG HEAVEN UNFAIR TO WOMEN and WOMENS RIGHTS NOW. Her attention is drawn to SKYE, a slender feminine protester with a blow horn. She has long straight blond hair in a headband and bell bottom pants. She's in her mid-late 20s.

                    SKYE
          Don't just stand there! Join us!

                    JR
          What are you protesting?

                    SKYE
          That demeaning poster inside! We're
          demanding that it be removed
          because it's offensive. You
          shouldn't be eating there.

JR walks with them for a bit and gets caught up in the chanting, clearly more interested in the women than the protest. Skye hands her a pamphlet.

                    SKYE (CONT'D)
          We have a women's meeting every
          Thursday night. You should join us,
          the big brown house on Temple.
          It'll do you good.

                    JR
          Oh, so it'll do me good? May have
          to check it out then. Is that the
          commune house?

                    SKYE
          We prefer to call it a collective.
          I'm Skye and you are..?

                    JR
          JR. And Skye? Like birds in the
          sky? Ok.

                    SKYE
             (with a teasing smile)
          7pm. Potluck. And bring some
          outrage if you've got any.

INT.BROWN HOUSE-EARLY EVENING

JR arrives at Skye's with a 6-pack of beer. ARLO, a hippie guy, opens the door and points her to the living room. Big pillows are on the floor, hanging plants, tapestries on the walls, incense burning and food on a low round table in the middle of the room. There are 5 other women and a couple of men. Folk music is playing.

                    SKYE
          Ok, time for you guys to go. Women
          only.

The women introduce themselves.

MAGIC, a hippie in beads and protest buttons. DEBBIE, a more conservatively dressed suburbanite in polyester. MAGGIE, an activist college student. JANINE, a working class housewife and VALERIE, a 30ish working professional woman.

                    SKYE (CONT'D)
          Skye. This is JR. What's your real
          name?

                         JR
               It's Jackie, Jacquelyn. But I
               prefer just JR.

                         MAGIC
               Names are very important. We need
               to reclaim ourselves and keeping
               our surnames perpetuates the belief
               that we are owned by our husbands
               and fathers. We can completely
               redefine ourselves by choosing our
               own names. Don't you think?

                         JR
               I just like it better, feels more
               like me.

                         MAGGIE
               I think it suits you. Are you a
               lesbian?

                         JR
                    (taken aback by the
                     directness)
               Yes.

The others glance over at Skye.

                         DEBBIE
               Ok then, JR. Who wants to start?

                         SKYE
               I'll go, I guess. My husband is
               still trying to keep my kids from
               me. He got his lawyer to say that
               I'm not a good mother because I
               left him.

                         JANINE
               That bastard. What? Does he really
               want to take care of them himself
               or does he just want to punish you?

                         SKYE
               I don't know, he's just so angry. I
               hate him but what can I do?

JR is surprised she has kids.

                         JR
               Isn't your lawyer working on that
               for you?

They all look at her.

                    JANINE
Um, lawyers cost money. Only those
with money have any power. You have
to give them a big retainer before
they'll do anything. Working people
don't get lawyers.

                    DEBBIE
And then if you do, you get a male
lawyer who says, oh, it's ok honey,
just accept what the court says.
Male lawyers, male judges. It would
be so different if women ran the
system! No one really advocates for
us.

                    JR
Public defenders can be appointed
to help if you can't afford one,
right?

                    VALERIE
That's only in criminal cases. My
husband got everything because I
didn't have anyone on my side.
You'll get your kids back, Skye.
They know you love them.

Arlo comes in very stoned to get some food from the table.

                    MAGIC
Arlo, did you not see the sign on
the door saying women's meeting?

                    ARLO
Just came to grab a bite. I'm not
staying.

                    MAGIC
Do you think you can find a way to
feed yourself without intruding on
us?

                    ARLO
Sorry. Can I have a beer?

                    JR
Sure.

                    SKYE
Out, Arlo!

                    MAGGIE
JR, tell us about yourself.

                    JR
This is my first time at a women's
meeting. Just in town for my
grandmother's funeral. I grew up
here but live in San Francisco now.
Uh, dropped out of college, not
sure what to do next.

                    VALERIE
Sorry about grandma, Do you want to
talk about it?

                    JR
Not really, it's .....
complicated.

The group nods in sympathy and support. A pause.

                    JANINE
When did you come out?

                    JR
Come out?

                    SKYE
Out of the closet, know when you
were gay?

                    JR
I've just always been out. Been a
tomboy jock all my life. I never
really thought about it, just
always knew I was different.

                    SKYE
Who else has anything they want to
talk about?

                    DEBBIE
I think we had a good turnout at
the Egg Heaven. They are
organizing in LA for a big ERA
rally. We have got to get women out
for this. Ideas? Ever been to a
protest march, JR?

                    VALERIE
         (before JR can answer)
Let me guess,...no... You grew up
in Palisades and your dad's a
lawyer.

>   JR
>   Actually I grew up in Belmont
>   Heights and what does my dad's work
>   have to do with anything?

>   JANINE
>   Our struggles are lost on some
>   folks who have had certain
>   advantages.

>   JR
>   You know nothing about my
>   struggles.

The group goes quiet.

>   MAGGIE
>   Generally speaking, of course. No
>   offense, JR. You're welcome here.
>   We need everyone to help keep the
>   attention on the ERA actions.

The discussion moves on. JR sits quietly in thought, taking in the conversations. The light changes as darkness falls outside. Food platters empty and the group starts to break up. As the others make their way out of the room, JR lingers behind.

>   SKYE
>   Thanks for coming, JR. So sorry
>   about your grandmother. Are you ok?

>   JR
>   (uncomfortable with the
>   question)
>   Yeah. Interesting group of women.
>   Gave me a lot to think about. I've
>   never been much of an activist.

After a pause.

>   SKYE
>   We need all the help we can get. We
>   all have to get mad and stay mad!

>   JR
>   You are absolutely right. Thank you
>   for inviting me.

They slowly walk to the door, both wanting to linger a little longer.

                    SKYE

          Can I ask you a favor? Could you
          give me a ride tomorrow to the
          park? I'm seeing my kids for my
          supervised visit and the bus
          connections are lousy.

                    JR
          Sure. So what's your real name,
          Ms. Skye?

                    SKYE
          Mary Ellen.

                    JR
          Skye suits you better, I think.
          See you tomorrow.

They exchange a long warm look.

INT.JR'S CAR-DAY

Skye bounces down the steps of the brown house and jumps in
the car.

                    JR
               (clearly happy to see her)
          Hey there.

                    SKYE
          Thanks so much for doing this. It
          really helps me out a lot. You know
          where the duck pond is in
          Recreation Park?

                    JR
          Sure. So how long have you been
          separated?

                    SKYE
          A year and it has been hell. I
          miss my kids so much. They came
          with me when I moved to the brown
          house but he hired an investigator
          to find me. Then the creep wrote
          up this report to the court about
          how I was living in some drug
          infested flop house.

                    JR
          Didn't seem so bad to me.

>   SKYE
>   A lot better than the suburban
>   prison I was trapped in before I
>   got out.

JR parks near where an older woman is waiting with 2 young
girls.

>   SKYE (CONT'D)
>   Oh, great, it's witch hazel, John's
>   mom. At least I won't have to see
>   him. You don't have to wait, I can
>   catch a bus to work from here.

>   JR
>   I can wait, just told a friend I
>   would drop by this afternoon.

EXT.PARK-DAY

The girls run to Skye. After they play on the swings awhile
Skye leads them back to witch hazel. They cling to Skye and
the younger one cries. JR watches from the car with curious
interest. Skye gets back into the car upset.

INT.JR'S CAR-DAY

>   JR
>   Your kids are beautiful, they look
>   just like you. Being a mom must be
>   really cool.

>   SKYE
>   They are, aren't they. It's the
>   hardest and most amazing thing
>   sometimes. I never knew I could
>   love so fierce until I held those
>   babies. How is it with you and your
>   mom?

>   JR
>   My mom died when I was 15.

>   SKYE
>   Yikes, that's ...harsh.

JR offers nothing further. A long silent moment passes.

                    JR
          Hey, if you don't need to get
          dropped off just yet, care to tag
          along while I visit my bartender
          friend?

                    SKYE
          Ok. I don't have to be to work for
          a couple of hours. I work at the
          Pancake House downtown.

                    JR
          I've eaten there before, usually at
          closing time after a night of
          drinking.

                    SKYE
          I see your kind almost every night
          but I'm only working until 10. Too
          weird after that.

JR starts the and drives away to pull up moments later in
front of Ripples Bar.

INT.RIPPLES BAR-DAY

Ripples is a trendy mens bar. There are several small groups
of men in conversations at the bar and nearby tables. JR and
Skye enter and sit near the order station. JR spots CAMERON,
a flamboyant African American man working behind the bar.

                    CAMERON
               (screaming in delight)
          Jackie Rae! The prodigal dyke
          returns! Come here, sister, I want
          to hear all about San Francisco.
          You home on break?

                    JR
          Nope, Grandma's funeral. Quit
          school last semester. This is Skye.

                    CAMERON
          Nice to meet you darlin. Aren't you
          pretty. And you, Jackie Rae,
          poor baby, you look like you could
          use a bloody mary.

                    JR
          Sure, I'll have one.

                    SKYE
          Not for me. Thanks. Just a coke.

Cameron signals to another bartender down the bar.

                    CAMERON
          You dropped out of school. I bet
          THAT went over well. (To Skye) This
          girl was the smartest one in our
          class. Her Daddy is one serious
          lawyer man.

                    JR
          San Francisco is beautiful, man.
          There are so many gay people moving
          there we've taken over a whole
          neighborhood.

                    CAMERON
          That's what I've heard and I got a
          friend there who says driving a cab
          is an easy job to get. I have GOT
          to get outta here. Take me back
          with you, PLEASE!

Cameron sets down Skye's coke and a giant bloody mary that
looks like a bouquet in front of JR. JR and Skye both start
laughing.

                    SKYE
          Now THAT'S a work of art.

                    CAMERON
              (pointing to the other
               bartender)
          Yes, literally! This is Art.

                    JR
          Cheers, man! Well done!

Art acknowledges the salute with flair.

                    JR (CONT'D)
          You'd leave Long Beach?

                    CAMERON
          Honey, I'd be out of here right now
          if I had $200 and a car. I got a
          friend in the Haight with an extra
          room. He's the cab driver.

                    JR
          A cab driver? I need to talk to him
          about that. You would take off just
          like that?

                    CAMERON
          Hell yeah, honey.

JR and Skye pick at the giant bloody mary chatting amicably
until Cameron returns from serving another customer.

                    JR
          So, I'm leaving in a couple of days
          and have room in my car, you wanta
          come?

                    CAMERON
          Oh, baby, Please, please! Are you
          serious?

                    JR
          Oh, baby, I'm serious.

Cameron squeals and jumps up and down.

                    CAMERON
          Two days?

                    JR
          Two days!

A young gay man rushes in screaming.

                    YOUNG GAY MAN
          BASHERS!

JR and two men at the bar rush out.

EXT.RIPPLES BAR-DAY

Three men are kicking another young man on the ground who is
screaming. They are young clean cut middle class college
kids. Skye, Cameron and a couple other patrons follow them.

                    JR
          Hey, get off him!

JR charges the nearest college kid and body slams him to the
pavement. The other two college kids stop as other bar
patrons pour into the parking lot. They begin to back away
then turn and flee.

JR is still wrestling the guy on the ground when BURLEY
PATRON joins her and delivers a quick hard kick to the guy's
ribs. He writhes in pain on the ground. Burley patron pins
him to the ground with his foot.

>   BURLEY PATRON
>   Thought you'd pick on some faggots
>   tonight?

Around the corner from the street a police car screeches to
a halt. The college kids who had just run away jump out of
the police car with the two cops.

>   COLLEGE KID 1
>   Over there. That's them. They
>   jumped us.

>   JR
>   You ganged up on him first. Three
>   against one. That's real brave!
>   They are the ones that should be
>   arrested!

>   COP
>   Alright, hold on there, break it
>   up. We'll decide what happened.

Cop 1 turns to the group and points to the man being held
down by Burley Patron.

>   COP 1
>   Let him up.

>   BURLEY PATRON
>   You gonna arrest them for
>   assaulting our friend over here?

>   COP 2
>   Let him up or I'll be arresting
>   everyone. Stand back both of you.

>   YOUNG GAY MAN
>   We did nothing to provoke them.
>   They tried to kill us!

Burly Patron takes his foot off the man's back. He and JR
slowly step back. The man on the ground stumbles to his feet
holding his side and joins his friends by the police car. A
crowd of bar patrons have gathered to join JR and Burley
Patron to face the police in a standoff.

>   CROWD OF PATRONS
>   Arrest those guys. Arrest them!

                    COP 1
          Shut up all of you and go back
          inside or we'll have this place
          shut down.

JR and Burley Patron hold their ground. Cop 2 pulls his
service revolver and aims it directly at JR. A tense moment
passed as JR stares him down. Skye gasps loudly.

                    JR
          And I thought our men in blue are
          here to serve and protect. What's
          your name, officer?

                    COP 2
          Get back inside, bull dyke, right
          now or we haul your ass in.

Cameron and Young Gay Man pull her back but Burley Patron
remains facing the officers in defiance. Another patron grabs
his shirt sleeve and he allows himself to be drawn back.

INT.RIPPLES BAR-NIGHT

Inside the bar patrons are agitated and the injured one is
being bandaged and consoled. JR angrily stomps to the bar,
slaps the bar stool and sits down to compose herself. Burley
Patron joins her on the next stool. Several others gather
around them. Skye is very frightened but tries to console JR.

                    PATRON 1
          I've seen those kids hanging around
          back there just hoping to get one
          of us alone, laughing and daring
          each other to pick a fight.

                    PATRON 2
          Thank you for standing up for us,
          that was amazing. You two are so
          brave! I thought you were going to
          get busted... or worse.

                    BURLEY PATRON
          I am so tired of the cops looking
          the other way. I only wish I could
          have hurt all three of them.

                    JR
          He pulled his service revolver on
          us! I'm going to report him!

                    ART
               (from the other side of
               the bar)
          Oh no, we are not making a fuss
          about this. The last thing I need
          is some trumped up reason for a
          raid or any other kind of police
          harassment. Just be grateful it
          ended the way it did.

                    CAMERON
          JR, I bout peed my pants when you
          stared that cop down and I am
          pretty sure the pig with the gun
          was about to lose his shit too.

                    JR
          They just defended those stupid
          college kids like it's ok to harass
          queers. That..is..not right!

                    ART
          Yeah, well, what else is new? Let
          it go, just let it go.

JR angrily shakes her head.

                    JR
          It's not right, it's just not
          right! How can you be ok with that?

                    ART
          Let it go. I don't want any trouble
          here.

Patron 1 claps her on the back to console her and the others
murmur their agreement with Art. After a few moments JR
remembers Skye is there with her.

                    JR
          You need to get to work, right?

Skye nods.

                    JR (CONT'D)
          I'll be back in a bit Cameron.

EXT.RIPPLES BAR-DAY

JR and Skye exit the bar and get into JR's car and drive off.
A few moments later they pull up at the Pancake House. JR is
still shaken.

                    SKYE
          That was so scary. I'm glad you
          didn't get hurt. But you are right
          to be angry. It's the same
          patriarchy that keeps women down
          that thinks it's ok to beat up gay
          people. They have the power but it
          is not right!

                    JR
          What can we do about it though?

They sit in silence for a moment.

                    SKYE
          You ok?

                    JR
          Yeah, I'm ok.

                    SKYE
          Oh, hey, I have something for you.

Skye pulls out a volume of Audre Lorde and copies of The
Ladder from her bag.

                    JR
          Looks like I have a bit of reading
          to do. Maybe I'll find some
          inspiration to help figure out the
          rest of my life.

                    SKYE
          I know exactly what that feels
          like! You aren't going back to San
          Francisco right away are you?

                    JR
          Staying around for a another day or
          so to see a couple more old friends
          before I leave.

                    SKYE
          Come by before you go back. I'd
          like to see you again and want to
          hear all about San Francisco.

                    JR
          I'd really like to see you too. You
          have an interesting life.

                          SKYE
                     (laughing)
                Thanks for that I guess!

Skye exits the car and then leans in to look at JR through
the window.

                          SKYE (CONT'D)
                You know, getting up in the face of
                a cop with a gun might get
                dangerous. We need the smart people
                people on the inside. Most of us
                can only make noise on the outside.

JR nods as Skye turns to walk away. JR watches her with an
approving smile on her face. Skye, also smiling, turns to
wave.

EXT.BROWN HOUSE-DAY

JR rings the bell. Cameron is waiting in the car at the curb.
Magic comes to the door.

                          JR
                Is Skye around?

                          MAGIC
                Don't think so.

Magic turns to speak to anyone in the house in earshot.

                          MAGIC (CONT'D)
                     (loudly)
                Anyone seen Skye today? Guess not.

                          JR
                I'm heading back to San Francisco
                and need to get on the road. I
                just wanted to say goodbye.

                          MAGIC
                Go by the restaurant. You know
                where she works? Hey and stop by
                the next time you are in town.

                          JR
                Thanks, I will.

INT.JR'S CAR-DAY

At the restaurant. JR goes in but comes right back out.

                    CAMERON
          Not there?

                    JR
          Nope, and no one knows if she's
          working later today.

                    CAMERON
          We gotta get on the road, honey.

JR is disappointed as they drive off and get to the freeway.

                    CAMERON (CONT'D)
          Here we go!! Woohoo!! I think from
          now on I shall be called Camomile.

                    JR
          I like that but I may have to keep
          it at Cam and don't call me Jackie.
          It's JR from here on out.

                    CAMERON
               (singing)
          San Francisco, open your golden
          gate, don't make nobody wait
          outside your door...

JR laughs and joins in.

Fog rolling in through the Golden Gate. Street scenes shift
to suggest the passing of time.

EXT.CAB STAND DOWNTOWN SAN FRANCISCO-DAY

1975. JR is driving a cab. She's in a slightly trendier but
still butch haircut and mens clothes.   Books on the seat,
disco on the radio. She's in a hotel line, studying when a
smartly dressed couple gets in her cab.

INT.JR'S CAB-DAY

                    JR
          Hello. Where to?

                    MALE PASSENGER
          Julius' Castle.

                    FEMALE PASSENGER
          We're on our honeymoon!

                          JR
                    (with exaggerated
                     giddiness)
          Well congratulations!

                    BOTH PASSENGERS
          Thank you!

JR starts the meter and pulls away. The passengers are eyeing
her from the back seat in curiosity.

                    MALE PASSENGER
          So, is this a good job for you? I
          think you are the first female cab
          driver I've seen.

                          JR
          I'm in school, it's flexible and
          not much of a distraction, ok for
          now.

                    FEMALE PASSENGER
          I thought you were a guy when we
          got in. So what's it like being a
          girl cab driver?

                          JR
                    (trying not to sound
                     annoyed)
          I've always been a girl so I can't
          really speak to what it's like
          being a guy cab driver.

Silence from the back seat. At the restaurant, the male
passenger pays with a large tip.

EXT.STREET-SAME DAY

JR drives away. Further down the next street she sees Arlo
and Skye. She is in her hippie attire and he has cut his hair
to more clean cut look. JR pulls up next to them.

                          JR
          Hey I know you guys, Skye!

                    SKYE
          For Real!! JR!

                          JR
          I never expected to see you here.

                    SKYE
          You remember Arlo, right?

                         JR
               For sure. I didn't recognize you in
               your new look, man. Get in, I'll
               give you a ride. What are you doing
               here?

INT.JR'S CAB-DAY

                         ARLO
               Part of our group just moved into a
               big victorian in the Haight. Skye
               is here for the Diablo Canyon No
               Nukes rally.

                         JR
               No kidding! I'm living in the
               Castro, we're almost neighbors.

                         SKYE
               The demonstration is this Saturday.
               They are building a nuclear power
               plant on an earthquake fault!

                         JR
               I know! Good for you for keepin the
               struggle alive! I'm working that
               day but will be there in spirit.
               You my dear are looking good.

Skye reaches over the seat to give JR a hug.

                         SKYE
               So are you. How things with you?

                         JR
               Great. I went back to school after
               all and just finishing my BA,
               waiting to hear if I get into law
               school.

                         SKYE
               Law school! That's a surprise!

                         JR
               Hey I looked for you the day I left
               to say goodbye but couldn't find
               you. I'm sorry. Wanted to see you
               before I left.

                    SKYE
I heard you came by. It would have
been nice to see you too but I had
to deal with custody stuff with my
ex.

                    JR
So that's all still going on?

                    SKYE
I lost my job at the restaurant
because the manager tried to corner
me in the back room. I had to push
him off me. When I complained the
owner just laughed. I told them
both they could go fuck themselves.

                    JR
Aughh. Good for you for standing up
to them.

                    SKYE
It got back to my ex-husband
somehow. I couldn't pay the court
fees and my visits got suspended.
I left right after that and went up
to Oregon for awhile. John of
course used this as more evidence
that I'm an 'unfit' parent. I've
just been kind of drifting since
then, seeing the girls whenever I
can.

                    JR
You did nothing wrong and they will
figure that out someday.

                    SKYE
Someday. Their stupid father thinks
Arlo is my lover and we are living
in sin.

                    JR
Anything that isn't mainstream and
middle class is inherently evil.

                    ARLO
Right on. I dig her girls, man, but
that guy would have me castrated or
something.

                    JR
Should have stayed a little longer,
maybe I could have helped somehow.

                         SKYE
              Maybe. Probably not, but I'm glad
              to see you now. Here you are,
              aspiring to be a lawyer, maybe
              that's your destiny after all.

                         JR
              I just want to do it on my own
              terms. There is civil rights work
              to be done and I want to be on the
              right side of it.

JR pulls the cab over at a corner in front of a large
victorian. Skye stays behind after Arlo gets out. JR refuses
payment.

                         JR (CONT'D)
              Is there anything I can do now? I
              mean, geez, how can I help?

                         SKYE
              No. Good luck with school. We need
              brave hearts like yours so stay on
              your path, Supergirl.

                         JR
              Maybe I'll see you tomorrow. Are
              you in town for awhile?

                         SKYE
              Probably leaving after the
              demonstration with the group I'm
              with. But I'll be back now that
              Arlo is here.

JR scribbles on a piece of paper and hands it to Skye.

                         JR
              Cool. Call me when you are back in
              town.

Skye reaches over the seat to give JR a hug and kiss on the
check before getting out of the cab. JR pulls away but
watches Skye in the rearview mirror. Skye lingers on the
sidewalk watching her drive away. They both sigh as they turn
away.

EXT.DEMONSTRATION-DAY

JR is cruising the periphery of the Stop Diablo Canyon
demonstration in her cab looking into the crowd. She is
disappointed as Skye is nowhere to be seen. Three gay men in
identical haircuts, mustaches and t-shirts get in.

                        PASSENGERS IN UNISON
            Kimos on Polk Street please.

                        JR
            You got it.

Montage

Lesbian Gay Pride Parade. Dykes on Bikes roar up the street.
JR is in the middle of the group as it stops. A young woman
in a bikini and a boa jumps on behind as the spectators cheer
and the bikers rev up to a deafening roar. It's a happy and
festive group. Disco music is blasting and the POV rises and
pulls back to show the size of the crown. Everyone is
joyful.

EXT.VALENCIA STREET-LATE AFTERNOON

JR backs her bike into a parking space in front of Amelia's,
a lesbian bar.

INT.AMELIA-SAME LATE AFTERNOON

JR bounces in with a letter in hand. She high-fives Cat at
the bar and says a few words then the small group at the bar
cheers.

Drinks and more congratulations are flowing. The disco crowd
is young and attractive. The music starts and the bar gets
crowded. JR's flirting and dancing with several women,
including SANDY, an attractive blond woman.

INT.JR'S APARTMENT-NIGHT

JR is on the couch, a little drunk, her hair is tousled and
she's wrapped in a bathrobe. She picks up the phone and dials
as Sandy kisses her on the forehead goodbye. JR waves with a
happy smile with a warm satisfied look.

                        JR
            Hey Dad, It's Jackie.

                        DAD (O.S.)
            Well, well, Jackie. We haven't
            heard from you for awhile.

                        JR
            I know, sorry. But I have some news
            I thought you might like to hear.

                    DAD (O.S.)
You're pregnant.

                    JR
NO, and I'm not getting married
either.

                    DAD (O.S.)
Ok, what?

                    JR
I got accepted for law school at
Golden Gate. I start this fall.

                    DAD (O.S.)
No kidding! I didn't know that was
in the plans.

                    JR
I didn't want to tell anyone until
it was a sure thing.

                    DAD
Where else did you apply? I mean,
did you try for Harvard or UCLA?

                    JR
I didn't apply outside of the bay
area. I want to stay in San
Francisco and do civil rights and
public interest law. There's some
great things happening here. I'm
canvassing for the Harvey Milk
campaign.

                    DAD (O.S.)
Is that the gay guy running for
office?

                    JR
Yes.

                    DAD (O.S.)
Civil Rights law? You want be one
of those troublemakers? How can
you make any money doing that?

                    JR
I'll find a way, I don't care about
that anyway.

                    DAD (O.S.)
Come here. Maybe we can get you
into UCLA.
                    (MORE)

                         DAD (O.S.) (CONT'D)
          We can find something interesting
          for you to work on. You and Mark
          can run the firm when I retire.

                         JR
          Not interested, Dad, and I'm sure
          Mark would do everything in his
          power to keep me out.

                         DAD (O.S.)
          You guys need to patch things up.
          We need to keep this family
          together. Why didn't you come to
          his wedding?

                         JR
          He and Barbie doll made it clear I
          was an embarrassment and not
          welcome.

                         DAD (O.S.)
          Your mom would be real proud to
          hear this, you know.

                         JR
          You must miss her a lot. I know it
          has been really hard for you and I
          get why you had to sell the house.

                         DAD (O.S.)
          Not sure she can be replaced. It's
          lonely being a widower at my age.

                         JR
          So go find yourself a young one.

                         DAD (O.S.)
               (sounding very sad)
          Maybe. I don't know.

Conversation pauses.

                         JR
          Well, I just wanted you to hear the
          news.

                         DAD (O.S.)
          I'm proud of you. Let me know if
          you need any help financially. You
          are quitting the cab job, right?

                         JR
          I'm ok. I have cheap rent and I
          like driving the cab.
                    (MORE)

                    JR (CONT'D)
          It's like real work with real
          people. Gotta do this on my own.

                    DAD (O.S.)
          Yeah, that's my girl.

INT.JR'S CAB-DAY

Three members of the Sisters of Perpetual Indulgence get into
the cab. Everyone is laughing, singing Fly Robin Fly and car
dancing.

EXT.STREET IN FRONT OF SCHOOL-DAY

JR roars up on her motorcycle.

INT.SCHOOL-DAY

JR walks in with her usual defiant swagger in army fatigues,
lesbian avenger t-shirt, and political buttons and carrying
her bike helmet. She passes the other students in much more
formal attire but acknowledges a couple of long-haired more
lefty looking students. She takes her place at a long table,
eager to take it on.

INT.SCHOOL LIBRARY-DAY

A library table is piles high with casebooks, JR is joined by
the other leftist students.

EXT.JR'S CAB-DAY

JR is sitting in the cab line at a hotel, dozing between
fares.

INT.SCHOOL OFFICE-DAY

JR is meeting with an academic advisor in her office who is a
very conservatively dressed middle aged woman. She's at her
desk looking over some papers.

                    ADVISOR
          What can I do for you, Ms. Benson?

                    JR
          I'm looking for a clerk position.

                         ADVISOR
              Your grades are certainly
              acceptable. Our placement office
              can help you with that. What is it
              you are interested in?

                         JR
              Any knd of civil rights work,
              domestic violence, housing
              discrimination.

                         ADVISOR
              There's not really a job title
              called 'civil rights lawyer.' Most
              firms just do a volunteer case here
              and there. Contact the Lawyers
              Guild, they have volunteer clinics
              for those issues.

                         JR
              Ok. I would still like to look
              through your referral list.

                         ADVISOR
                    (hesitating a moment)
              Your chances would be improved if
              you could dress a little more
              professional. And I appreciate
              your... individuality, but you need
              to be a little more...conforming.

                         JR
                    (barely hiding her
                    disdain)
              Thanks for the advice.

INT.MISSION LEGAL CLINIC-DAY

The clinic is a storefront in a run down neighborhood next to
a laundromat. JR is being interviewed by the managing
attorney, RAYMOND, who is frazzled and scruffy looking. He's
in his 50s.

                         RAYMOND
              Welcome to the fray, Ms.
              Jacquelyn...

                         JR
              JR.

                         RAYMOND
              Sorry?

                        JR
          Just JR.

                        RAYMOND
          Ok, then, just JR, we'll have you
          working on housing complaints that
          need to be investigated. Basically
          you'll be doing intake interviews
          and some limited investigation.

                        JR
          Why only limited investigation?

                        RAYMOND
          Because we don't have enough
          people. You see that pile of
          files? That's the housing caseload.
          We can only really work on the most
          serious cases. So pace yourself.
          Good luck.

INT.SCHOOL LIBRARY-DAY

Montage

JR with the study group who, frame by frame, over time cut
their hair, shave their beards and shift their appearances to
more professional looks. JR's look shifts only a little from
army fatigues to jeans. She still maintains her butch profile
and swagger.

INT.AUDITORIUM-DAY

Graduation. As JR walks across the stage to receive her
degree, the POV pans to the audience to show flamboyant
Cameron, Cat, Sandy and Dad.

TV NEWS REPORTS MONTAGE

Another large gay pride celebration.

Harvey Milk is giving his "Gotta Give Them Hope" speech.

INT.JR'S CAB-DAY

A lesbian couple gets in the cab laughing and immediately
start making out in the back seat. JR drives away smiling.

Next fare.

A straight couple gets in, obviously mad at each other.
Neither are speaking as JR drives away. They pass an older
hippie lady on the street in tie dye and lots of flowers.

                    JR
          Oh look! It's Cosmic Lady!

The couple in the back seat ignore her and stare out their
windows without responding. Cosmic lady acknowledges JR with
a bow.

Next fare.

Sandy gets in. JR drives away pretending not to recognize
her.

                    JR (CONT'D)
          Hey gorgeous, where to?

                    SANDY
          Hey gorgeous, yourself. I think you
          know where I live.

                    JR
          Believe I do. What's for dinner
          tonight?

                    SANDY
          You'll see. Don't be late.

EXT.JR'S APT-DAY

JR walks up to the door with a bouquet of flowers that say
Happy Anniversary.

INT.JR'S APT-DAY

As JR opens the door and enters the lights go on and is
greeted by Cat and several other women who all yell SURPRISE.
JR is laughing as Sandy greets her with a hug. The music
starts with Chris Williamson singing Song of the Soul as the
group gathers around a buffet, mingling and filling their
plates. Cat starts pouring champagne and toasting. They all
join in the chorus.

EXT.CASTRO CAMERA-EVE

Signage on a storefront window reads Castro Camera and Harvey
Milk Campaign Headquarters. A crowd is gathering inside. JR
in her cab stops out front to let out two gay passengers.

                    JR
          I'm passing out safety whistles for
          our neighborhood watch group. Need
          one?

                    PASSENGER 1
          Got ours. Prop 8 and Harvey
          debating Briggs is bringing the
          creeps out in full force. We all
          need to do our part.

JR and the passengers take out the whistles and toot them
simultaneously with a laugh. The passengers go inside.

JR waits outside the camera store. The crowd inside is
cheering as Harvey Milk addresses them. She smiles with pride
as the energy of the chanting spills into the street.

INT.JR'S APARTMENT-NIGHT

Sandy and JR are having dinner.

                    SANDY
          Big interview this week. Are you
          excited?

                    JR
          I AM! Small progressive firm with
          three women attorneys. It's
          perfect. You know it is so amazing
          to think that Harvey could actually
          be the first openly gay elected
          official in the country. I mean
          think about it, the world will
          never be the same no matter what
          happens.

                    SANDY
          I hear he's gotten death threats.

                    JR
          Yes, he has but he's carrying on
          because it's the right thing to do.
          To stand up to the world like this.
          We're here and we are not going
          away!!

                    SANDY
          Do you think he's really got a
          chance?

                    JR
He'll have to get a lot of straight
people to vote for him. He says if
everyone came out to their families
and co workers everyone would know
a gay person AND that we aren't all
monsters and child molesters.

                    SANDY
I could never come out at work.
It's too dangerous. He is stirring
up so much hate. I could only tell
people I'm very close to. Better to
just blend in, I can't lose this
job.

                    JR
I could never just blend in and I'm
pretty sure everyone in my family
has known since I was eight and
wanted to wear boxers. My parents
had no idea what to do with me.

                    SANDY
          (laughing)
You wanted to wear boys underwear?
Didn't go over so well, I take it.

                    JR
No. It did not go over well.

INT.SUBURBAN HOME-NIGHT FLASHBACK

JR as a eight year old in pajamas is hiding behind a hallway
corner outside her parents' bedroom. They are arguing behind
the closed door.

                    MOTHER (O.S.)
I can't stand this anymore, we
can't just let her do whatever she
wants. She is NOT a boy! We have to
nip this in the bud now before she
gets any older.

                    FATHER (O.S.)
She'll be ok. It's just a phase.

                    MOTHER (O.S.)
It's more than a phase, there is
something seriously wrong with her
and I want her to see a
psychiatrist.

                         FATHER (O.S.)
          We will do nothing of the sort.
          She's just fine the way she is. End
          of conversation.

EXT.RESIDENTIAL STREET-NIGHT

JR is walking alone on a dark street. A late model sedan
drives by slowly and stops, blocking her path as she starts
across. The windows are down and there are 3 or 4 young men
inside

                         YOUNG MAN 1
          Hey, faggot, where ya going?

                         JR
          To my house right there.

                         YOUNG MAN 2
          Well, well! It's not a faggot but a
          dyke.

The others laugh. JR bends down to peer inside the car.

                         JR
          Yeah, and what's your point?

Laughter stops. JR blows her whistle and the car speeds away.

EXT.ARLO'S HAIGHT VICTORIAN-DAY

JR in her cab drives slowly past Arlo's house and she slows
to a stop to look at the house when a young woman taps on the
window.

                         YOUNG WOMAN
          Hi, are you free?

                         JR
          Yes, hop in.

The woman gets in the cab, and JR looks back at the house
before driving on.

INT.JR'S APARTMENT-DAY

JR bursts in through the door. Sandy is sitting on the couch
reading a book.

                    SANDY
          There she is. So the interview went
          well?

JR drops her jacket and backpack and plops down next to her.

                    JR
          YES! I met the partners, JEFFREY
          and his wife MARCIA and the other
          two women attorneys. Very liberal
          politics. And they are real
          interested in hiring me. Said
          they'd get back to me with
          something in a day or so.

                    SANDY
          What does 'something' mean?

                    JR
          It's a small firm. They are
          probably trying to figure out what
          to pay me. But anything has got to
          better than what I'm making driving
          a cab.

                    SANDY
          They have to offer you something
          worthwhile. You have that big
          downtown firm interview coming up
          too. Wouldn't that be a more
          prestigious place to start? I'll
          take you to Nordstroms to find a
          really nice suit for you to wear.

                    JR
          I don't want to work for a big firm
          doing just whatever. Corporate
          contracts, divorces, property
          owners screwing over their tenants.
          These guys actually do some great
          civil rights work, like that
          housing class action and the weekly
          low income law clinic volunteer
          work they send their people to work
          at. That's why I went to law
          school.

                    SANDY
          It would be great to have some real
          money coming in. We could move out
          of this little place, maybe get a
          new car.
                    (MORE)

SANDY (CONT'D)
There's a beautiful flat coming up
for rent on Liberty street that I
would love to go look at.

JR
(ignoring her)
I need to go by Harvey's campaign
headquarters this afternoon, the
campaign is really picking up
steam. He's getting so much
attention these days.

SANDY
How did we get from your job
prospects to Harvey?

JR
There is so much to do!

SANDY
So you've made up your mind to
accept whatever they offer? You
know if it was a really good
salary, my grandmother might help
with a downpayment for a house.

JR
I know. I know. They asked me if I
had other lawyers in my family.
They had actually heard of Dad's
firm and wanted to know if I would
leave the area to go back to work
there.

SANDY
Would that really be so bad, JR?
We'd be in the money for sure if
you did. What did you say?

JR
(thinking a moment)
I can't imagine ever doing the kind
of work they do. My life is here in
San Francisco.

JR takes Sandy's book away and throws it over her shoulder.
They embrace and laugh, pulling at each other's clothes.

EXT.CASTRO STREET-LATE AFTERNOON

The street is packed with people. A TV visible from the
street through an open bar window is broadcasting election
results. Briggs loses, Milk wins. The onlookers cheer and
it starts to rain.

INT.CASTRO CAMERA-SAME TIME

JR, Sandy and Cat are in the crowd to watch the election
results. A TV mounted high on the wall is also broadcasting
the results and the crowd is cheering.

                    CROWD
          SPEECH SPEECH SPEECH

Harvey Milk climbs up on a table and raises his arms.

                    HARVEY MILK
               WE DID IT!! The Briggs initiative
               is defeated! Mr. Briggs, it looks
               like gay people in California have
               a lot of friends!

The crowd cheers.

                    HARVEY MILK (CONT'D)
               And look, it's raining! Anita
               Bryant has been saying the
               California drought is because of
               all those awful gay people out
               here. What do think of this,
               Anita!

The crowd cheers.

INT.JR'S OFFICE-DAY

A modest office in an old victorian. JR comes in wearing a
tailored pantsuit and with a beat up briefcase. Her look is
less butch and more androgynous. She closes her office door,
reopening it after changing into jeans and a flannel shirt.
The receptionist, ROSE, is a younger 'alternative' looking
woman with dyed black hair and army boots.

                    ROSE
               Feel better?

                    JR
               You have no idea.

                         ROSE
             I got a pretty good idea.

They exchange a look of mutual respect.

                         JR
             I'm glad you're here.

INT.JR'S OFFICE-DAY

Attorney MARCIA taps on the door carrying an arm load of
files. She is in her late 30's, stylish but conservatively
dressed.

                         MARCIA
             So, how'd it go?

                         JR
             It got referred to arbitration,
             just like you said it would.

                         MARCIA
             Ok so I have a few insurance files
             I'd like you to look over. Maybe
             just write up a short memo on each
             with a facts and liability
             analysis.

                         JR
             That shouldn't take too long. Ok if
             I head over to the shelter around
             4? They are doing their restraining
             order clinic there tonight and I
             think there will be a couple of
             women that need some help.

                         MARCIA
             Sure, as long as this is all done.

                         JR
             It will be.

                         MARCIA
             One more thing. We would like to
             market the firm on a few more
             referral panels. Any chance you's
             be willing to use your formal name
             Jacquelyn instead of JR? That way
             people won't think you are a guy.
             It's a little confusing and we'd
             look more like the 'womens' firm
             that we really are. Just for the
             sake of clarity.

                         JR
                    (sighs)
               I'll think about it but would
               prefer to keep it at JR because
               it's who I am. Jeffrey's not
               leaving is he? We're still a mostly
               'womens' firm.

                         MARCIA
               That's fine, just thought I would
               ask. I respect your choice.

                         JR
               Thank you Marcia. It's important to
               me.

EXT.ANGELS HOUSE WOMENS SHELTER-DAY

A large older house in a rundown neighborhood, trash in the
street, a homeless person is sleeping in a doorway.

INT.ANGELS HOUSE WOMENS SHELTER-DAY

JR and CARMEN, a worn out young Latina woman with two kids
emerge from a small office. The girl, LUCY, about 7 looks at
JR as a young boy, ROMAN, holds a toy truck without making
eye contact.

                         CARMEN
               God knows, I'm trying my best.

                         JR
               I know you are and you've gotten
               yourself out of that situation so
               things are looking up, right? I'll
               get this filed and we'll get this
               restraining order in place in the
               next day or so.

                         CARMEN
               Thank you so much.

The young girl waves to her as JR moves toward the door. JR
returns the wave with a smile. Several other women and their
children in the shabby common room are watching TV,
spellbound. It's the early news coverage of the Jonestown
Peoples Temple mass suicide. JR stops to watch.

                         HOUSE MANAGER
               My auntie went to that church
               before they moved it to that Guyana
               place.
                    (MORE)

                    HOUSE MANAGER (CONT'D)
          Thank goodness she didn't go with
          them. So many insane things happen
          in San Francisco.

Several other women nod in agreement.

                    WOMAN RESIDENT
          This is one crazy town for sure.

INT.JR'S CAR-DAY

JR is driving away from the shelter when she starts to space
out. The television images of the bodies at Jonestown
resurface. She pulls over to the curb to calm her nerves.
Another faint image of a body floating in a pool briefly
surfaces. She blinks and shakes her head to compose herself.

INT.CITY HALL-DAY

JR and Carmen are leaving a courtroom.

                    JR
          I know it was hard for you to give
          that testimony but you did great.
          He will be served by a police
          officer very soon. Are you sure he
          doesn't know where you and the kids
          are now?

                    CARMEN
          I'm pretty sure he doesn't know and
          I've been careful not to tell
          anyone.

                    JR
          You need to get back there as soon
          as you can. I'll drive you but
          you'll need to lay low for awhile.
          Ok? Maybe send the kids to stay
          with someone you trust that lives
          out of town.

Shouting and people are rushing by.

                    JR (CONT'D)
          What's going on?

                    POLICE OFFICER
          There's been a shooting, we need to
          clear the building.

JR and Carmen hurry out. Police are directing people to disperse.

INT.JR'S OFFICE-DAY

The phones are ringing but everyone is gathered around a small TV in the conference room.

>   JR
>   There's been a shooting at City
>   Hall.

>   MARCIA
>   We just heard.

The news cameras break to a podium where Dianne Feinstein announces that Harvey Milk and Mayor George Moscone have been shot and killed by Supervisor Dan White.

JR sinks into a chair, stunned. She calls Sandy.

>   JR
>   Sandy turn on the TV. Harvey's been
>   shot!

>   SANDY (O.S.)
>   I just heard. Weren't you in court
>   today with that restraining order
>   case?

>   JR
>   Yes, they rushed us out of the
>   building, I just got back to the
>   office.

>   MARCIA
>   JR, I'm so sorry. This is so
>   terrible, are you ok?

>   JR
>   (screaming in disbelief)
>   Dan White!   DAN WHITE!!!

Everyone in the office is expressing their shock and disbelief as JR stares off into space.

INT.JR'S APARTMENT-DAY

JR is staring out the window in profile. TV news coverage is reflected on the glass showing the draped bodies being removed from City Hall. She sips at a cocktail.

EXT.SUBURBAN HOME-DAY FLASHBACK

JR as a 15 year old in a softball uniform is watching from
the second story window in profile as a draped body is being
removed from her home. An ambulance is waiting at the curb
but no one is hurrying. The scene fades.

INT.JR'S APARTMENT-DAY FLASH FORWARD

Sandy comes up behind her and wraps her arms around JR and
they slowly rock. Tears are rolling down JR's face.

EXT.MARKET STREET-TWILIGHT

JR and Sandy join the large crowd of people walking silently
up the street at dusk. Someone hands them each a candle in a
paper up as the join the walk. JR's face moves from sadness
to anger.

Footage of the Candlelight March to City Hall. Holly Near is
singing "We Are Singing for Our Lives."

EXT.ANGELS HOUSE WOMENS SHELTER-NIGHT

A cab waits at the curb as Carmen and her two kids emerge
from a side door. The kids get in.

INT.CAB-NIGHT

Carmen speaks through the window.

                    CARMEN
          You guys, the cab is going to take
          you to the bus station where Tio
          Sergio is going to ride you to
          Sacramento, ok? You are going to
          stay with Josefa's abuela. They are
          gonna call me when you get there.
          It's gonna be ok.

Roman starts to cry softly.

                    LUCY
          Mama, why can't you come too? Papa
          might find you.

                    CARMEN
          Mijo, don't cry. I need you guys to
          be brave. It's gonna be ok.
                    (MORE)

                    CARMEN (CONT'D)
          I promise. Look at me both of you.
          Be brave, ok?

                    LUCY AND ROMAN
          Ok Mama.

Carmen steps back as the cab pulls away. She brushes back
tears, pulls her red jacket tighter and turns to go back into
the house. Across the street in a dark van, a man watches.
He starts the car to follow the cab just as a police car
drives slowly by. He hesitates a moment and then shuts off
the engine.

INT.ANGELS HOUSE-DAY

JR comes into the common room. The women are crying. The
house manager meets her.

                    JR
          What's up? Did something happen?

                    HOUSE MANAGER
          Yes, JR. Carmen sent her kids off
          to Sacramento last night and they
          got there safe. But her husband
          caught her when she went to take
          the garbage out this morning. He
          convinced her to get in his van by
          saying he knew where the kids were.
          We tried to get the license number
          before they drove away but
          couldn't. The police are looking
          for them now.

                    ANOTHER RESIDENT
                (Distraught)
          It's all my fault. I should have
          been the one to go outside.

                    HOUSE MANAGER
          It's no one's fault. All we can do
          is pray he won't hurt her.

                    JR
                (outraged)
          We have a restraining order, the
          guy will go to jail. If he hurts
          her he will do serious time. We'll
          get him and he will go to jail.

Through the window, a police car pulls up and two officers
emerge. One of them is holding Carmen's red jacket.

                              HOUSE MANAGER
                  Oh, no. Everyone upstairs.

The women leave the room as the officers come inside.

                              JR
                  I'm JR Bensen, Carmen's attorney.
                  Have you found her?

                              OFFICER 1
                  If this is her jacket then yes. It
                  was in a van that went off the road
                  on Hwy 1. Both people in the van
                  are deceased. We're checking IDs
                  now.

                              JR
                  We had a restraining order! You
                  guys were supposed to protect her!!

                              HOUSE MANAGER
                  Then the kids weren't with them?

                              OFFICER 2
                  No, ma'am. Only two adults were in
                  the van.

                              JR
                       (more outraged)
                  WE HAD A RESTRAINING ORDER!! This
                  should not have happened!

                              OFFICER 1
                  We were patrolling the street, we
                  can't be everywhere, Ms. Bensen.

JR's vision blurs and a roaring sound begins to arise as the
room starts to swirl. She turns toward the window to gather
herself.

INT.JR'S CAR-DAY

JR is driving away. She lingers too long at a light and the
car behind her honks, startling her. Her hands are shaking
and she is struggling to stay focused. She catches her
breath and her face hardens.

EXT.STREET-TWILIGHT

JR, weary and preoccupied, walks up to the front of her house
but stops to look at her motorcycle for a moment.

She goes in to return in a leather jacket and carrying her helmet. She decides against the helmet and leaves it on the step. She gets on, revs the engine and speeds down the street.

EXT-WINDING COASTAL ROAD-TWILIGHT

JR is speeding along the road and pulls over at a scenic overlook. She looks over the steep cliff to the waves crashing below for a moment, taking deep breathes to calm herself. Then she shuts off the engine and turns her view to the setting sun.

SEVERAL MONTHS LATER

Time-lapse of City Hall with the sky changing and clouds moving swiftly casting shadows on the dome of the building.

INT.JR'S OFFICE-DAY

JR packs her briefcase. She is in a slightly more professional look but still wears her hair short and her suit has a fashionable but distinctly masculine cut to it. She has an angry harder look.

EXT.STREET-DAY

JR passes a newsstand. Headlines read JURY STILL OUT IN DAN WHITE MURDER TRIAL and DEFENSE RESTS AFTER ARGUING THE TWINKIE DEFENSE.

INT.JR'S APARTMENT-DAY

JR in street clothes, with a drink. Cat is there. The TV news reports that Dan White is acquitted of the murder charge and found guilty of the lesser charge of involuntary manslaughter.

                    JR
          WHAT!! That cannot be possible, it
          was premeditated! NO! WHAT??

Sandy looks in from the kitchen.

                    CAT
          That's unbelievable. Because he ate
          junk food and lost his mind? That
          is crazy!

                    JR
          This is going to be trouble. They
          are probably gathering at City Hall
          right now. I had better get over
          there.

                    SANDY
          Why do you need to go? Dinner is
          going to be ready in a few minutes.
          Stay here.

                    CAT
          JR, Sandy just made dinner. I'll go
          with you in awhile if you still
          want to go. Calm down, JR.

                    JR
          I have to go.

                    SANDY
          You don't have to go, JR!

JR grabs a jacket and heads for the door. Cat and Sandy
exchange a look of helplessness.

                    CAT
          Wait. I'm coming with you.

EXT.CITY HALL-TWILIGHT

                    CROWD
          HE GOT AWAY WITH MURDER! DAN WHITE
          MUST DIE!

Cat and JR make their way to the front of the crowd at City
Hall. A few police are there. Restless protesters are
starting to throw rocks at the building windows. An official
with a blow horn is on the second story balcony overlooking
the crowd.

                    OFFICIAL
          Please stay calm. There is no need
          for violence. We understand your
          anger.

                    JR
          NO MORE VIOLENCE! JUST STAND! STAY
          CALM STAY CALM. NO MORE VIOLENCE!

Two men continue to throw rocks and objects at the glass
doors. Police are visible inside the building. JR and Cat
try pulling the others back but they are resisting.

Then from behind her several police in riot gear rush the steps and start clubbing. A camera flashes just as JR and Cat start to run. JR stumbles trying to get away and is hit in the head as she gets up again. Cat grabs her and pulls her away as she tries to stay on her feet.

                    JR (CONT'D)
          STOP! STOP!

                    CAT
          JR we gotta get out of here!

The crowd seeing the police clubbing the demonstrators start taunting the police and throwing things at them. Chaos erupts with the sound of breaking glass. There is screaming and chants of DAN WHITE MUST DIE. Tear gas fills the air. JR is stumbling as they try to get away.

                    CAT (CONT'D)
          HELP ME!

A male and a female demonstrator come to their aid as JR slips to the ground. The sirens are coming from all directions as reinforcements arrive and people are running in all directions. They drag carry JR through the crowd and flag down a cab.

INT.JR'S APARTMENT-NIGHT

Sandy paces, watching the riot live on TV. She calls Marcia.

                    SANDY
               (near hysterical)
          Marcia, JR and Cat are out there in
          that crowd. Now they are saying the
          police cars are on fire and people
          are getting beat up!

                    MARCIA (O.S.)
          We're watching it too. I'm sure
          they will be ok. Let me know if you
          don't hear from them.

Sandy hangs up. The phone rings.

INT.HOSPITAL ER-NIGHT

Cat is at a pay phone in the hospital. It is noisy and very busy. She has to cover one ear to speak into the phone.

                    CAT
          Sandy, JR got hurt. We're at St.
          Mary's.

                    SANDY (O.S.)
          Oh my god. Is she ok? I'll be
          right over there.

                    CAT
          She's a little woozy, I think they
          want to keep her here overnight.
          She got hit in the head.

EXT.STREET IN FRONT OF THE HOSPITAL ER-NIGHT

There are ambulances and other vehicles coming in and people
are being helped out of cars.

INT.HOSPITAL ER-NIGHT

Sandy and Marcia find JR and Cat in the chaotic ER with
several other beat up demonstrators. JR has a bandage over
the side of her head and there is blood on the front of her
clothes.

                    SANDY
                 (angrily)
          JR, what were you thinking!

                    JR
                 (very agitated)
          The cops were beating everybody
          including us and we were just
          trying to calm everyone down. The
          crowd went nuts!

                    MARCIA
          Calm down JR. Did you get hurt
          anywhere else?

                    JR
                 (almost screaming)
          We have to talk to these people
          here and get their statements. They
          are all witnesses. We need to do
          this now!

A doctor and a nurse come in.

>   DOCTOR
> You need to calm down. Your x-rays
> look ok but you're staying
> overnight for observation. One of
> you can stay but the rest need to
> leave.

>   JR
> We have to get their statements.
> They are witnesses!

Cat, Marcia and Sandy wait outside the room.

>   SANDY
>   (frustrated and angry)
> Cat, thank you so much for being
> there. I can't believe this
> happened. I tried to get her to
> stay home.

>   CAT
> Well, you know our supergirl JR is
> not going to stay out of a fight.
> She'll be ok and you know she is
> going to want to make a big deal
> out of this.

>   MARCIA
> I know. That's what I'm afraid of.

INT.JR'S OFFICE-DAY

Office staff meeting. JR has an ugly bruise on the side of
her face. A copy of the SF Examiner is on the table with a
photo of JR being knocked down by the police on the front
page. The headline reads RIOT AFTER WHITE VERDICT. JEFFREY,
Marcia's husband is leading the meeting. He is in his late
30's and a bit of a 70's dandy with coiffed hair and a bow
tie. Marcia as well as several other staff listen.

>   JR
> We need to talk about what happened
> last week and how this firm might
> be able to take some of these
> police brutality claims. They need
> to be held accountable.

>   JEFFREY
> We are stretched pretty thin as it
> is. Susan has a trial coming up
> next week and we are swamped with
> all the new insurance work we are
> starting to get.

                    MARCIA
I love your idea JR and I know
you've spent a lot of time talking
to people but it's taking you away
from work we need to get into here.
How many declarations have you
taken so far?

                    JR
I've talked to over 20 people who
sustained some type of injury at
the hands of the police that night
and dozens more who are willing to
be witnesses.

                    JEFFREY
Aside from individual claims
against the police, how do you
really see this going forward, JR?

                    JR
We need to make a lot of noise! A
class action, maybe. A grand jury
investigation, charges against the
individual officers. They went to
Castro Street after they left City
Hall, trashed a bar and beat up
people just sitting there having a
drink.

                    MARCIA
And apparently had their badges
covered so they couldn't be
identified. How will we be able to
name them?

                    JEFFREY
I love your passion, JR, but aside
from handling individual claims, I
don't know what resources we can
bring to this. I have no objections
to you working on this on your own
time, but we have work here that
needs your attention during
business hours.

                    JR
C'mon, Jeff, and Marcia, how can
you let this go? We have to do
something. Can we at least try and
get these cases consolidated so the
police have to answer for this as a
department?

                        JEFFREY
          File your motion for consolidation,
          but if it's not allowed, we can't
          pursue this any further. That's the
          best we can do. We can't just do
          all this free legal work and stay
          in business.

JR storms out of the office.

EXT.JR'S OFFICE-DAY

Around the corner from the office she leans against a wall to
steady herself and the roar in her head starts to subside.
After a few moments she heads back into the office.

INT.JR'S OFFICE-DAY

JR walks through the office without speaking and goes to her
desk. Rose appears at her office door.

                        ROSE
          Hey, you ok?

                        JR
          Sorry. Did I miss anything?

                        ROSE
          Nothing worthwhile. Oh, this came
          for you. I opened it by mistake. Is
          this your brother? Weren't they
          just here a couple weeks ago?

It's a framed photo of JR with Mark and his family walking on
a beach. A smiling JR is holding the hand of a little girl in
a frilly dress who is looking up at her.

                        JR
          Mark was in town on business so he
          brought the whole family. That's
          Barbara, his wife, Sonja, Peter and
          the baby is Brenda. I think he was
          trying to make peace by showing me
          his kids.

                        ROSE
          Did it work?

                        JR
          He's finally getting over who I am.
          That's a big step for him.
                        (MORE)

                    JR (CONT'D)
          That Sonja is a sassy little thing.
          I like being the auntie.

INT.UPSCALE NEIGHBORHOOD BAR-DAY

JR is drinking by herself. Jeffrey comes in and sits next to
her. He motions to the bartender who knows what he wants. A
moment passes with neither of them speaking. Jeffrey
patiently waits for her to speak.

                    JR
          The motion to consolidate was
          denied.

                    JEFFREY
          You gave it a good shot, and you
          know it isn't always going to go
          your way.

                    JR
          I can't help wondering how I could
          have made a better argument.

                    JEFFREY
          You made the best case you could
          and everyone knows the White
          verdict was outrageous. But that
          just goes to show how the public
          supports the police. They are the
          good guys, remember?

                    JR
          It's just so wrong.

                    JEFFREY
          Yes, but I have something that may
          cheer you up a little. It's an
          invitation to the San Francisco Bar
          Association awards dinner next
          week.

                    JR
          I don't have to go do I? I hate
          those kinds of things.

                    JEFFREY
          You might want to. They've
          announced that "the Law Offices of
          Patterson & Barrett, with special
          recognition of JR Bensen, Attorney
          at Law, has been awarded the Pro
          Bono Attorneys of the Year award
          for their tireless work on housing
          issues, the Angel House Restraining
          Order clinic and service to the
          legal needs of underrepresented
          citizens of San Francisco."

                    JR
          That's kinda....cool.

                    JEFFREY
          Congratulations. You know, I
          started out with the kind of
          idealism that you have.

                    JR
               (annoyed)
          Yeah, so what happened?

                    JEFFREY
          Life happened. A mortgage, a
          family. I had to grow up. Being
          comfortable is not so bad.

                    JR
               (more annoyed)
          I grew up 'comfortable' where the
          only thing that mattered was money
          and some imaginary perfect life
          that nothing to do with the real
          world. I don't need to do
          'comfortable'.

                    JEFFREY
          How does Sandy feel about that?
          It's all about balance, JR. Don't
          make yourself crazy. You don't need
          to stand up for every lost cause.
          We can't really change the world.

She stands to face Jeffrey directly.

                    JR
          And we can't just sell out. I know
          what it means to stand up for
          someone else because someone stood
          up for me.

JR gets up to leave.

                    JEFFREY
                (defensively)
           I didn't sell out.

JR turns and walks away.

                JEFFREY (CONT'D)
              (to the bartender)
           She'll come around.

DREAM SEQUENCE

Out of focus images of people falling through space, muffled
voices. "It's all your fault, you have to fix this, you don't
care about anyone but yourself." The images briefly sharpen
into the face of her mother. "You don't care about anyone
else". The roaring sound starts to rise and the image of a
wrecked dark van being pulled from a ravine fades in.

INT.JR'S BEDROOM-NIGHT

JR sits upright in bed panting, disoriented and sobbing.

                SANDY
           What is it? What's going on?

                JR
              (calming herself)
           Just a dream. Go back to sleep.

JR gets up and goes into the kitchen and pours herself a
bourbon. Her hands are shaking. A few minutes later Sandy
comes in, sits down and takes JR's hands.

                SANDY
           So what's the dream about? Is it
           the same one that woke you up the
           other night?

                JR
           It's not about anything. Just
           sounds and voices, angry voices. I
           can't really make out who they are.
           Mom was talking, I think.

                SANDY
           Maybe it would be good to talk to
           someone about your mom.

                        JR
          I've had almost as much therapy
          about her as she's had about me.
          Not going there again.

                        SANDY
          You know what happened to Carmen
          was not your fault.

INT.JR'S BEDROOM-NIGHT

Sandy leads her back to the bed and wraps JR in her arms. JR
is wide awake staring at the ceiling.

INT.SUBURBAN HOME-DAY FLASHBACK

JR is 15, very short hair in a softball uniform, walks
through her house to the back patio to find her mother
floating face down in the pool.

                        JR
              MOM! MOM!

EXT.CITY SCENE-DAY
The fog is rolling over Twin Peaks followed by a shot looking
down Castro Street.

INT.OFFICE-DAY

Another office staff meeting with several people around a big
table. JR comes in late, hungover. Marcia is annoyed.

                        JEFFREY
          So assignments for the new work
          will be out later today. Who needs
          help on what they are working on
          right now?

                        JR
          I was at the Mission Legal Clinic
          office yesterday and there has been
          a huge rise in the number of
          evictions lately that they need
          help with. This gay cancer has a
          lot of landlords afraid and sick
          guys are getting kicked out of
          their homes.

                    MARCIA
          Sorry, JR. We need your focus here
          and for you to be doing more than
          just writing case reviews now that
          we are getting all this insurance
          work.

                    JR
          I knew you would say that. These
          housing cases are important. I
          have to say I am real disappointed.
          I came to this firm because you had
          the best ethics and the best record
          for doing civil rights work and now
          you are only interested in this
          insurance shit.

                    JEFFREY
          We have done our share of impact
          work, JR, and you have done a
          fantastic job AND we have
          tremendous respect for your
          compassion and your enthusiasm but
          this is a business. We have to make
          some money too.

                    MARCIA
          You could be making a lot more
          money, JR, if we could share more
          of the fees on these cases. You
          need to be doing your part to bring
          in the clients to keep us going.

                    JR
          This disease is killing gay men at
          an unprecedented rate. There is
          genuine panic out there. These are
          people who are being disowned by
          their families because they had to
          come out when they got sick.

                    JEFFREY
          Ok, this meeting is over. JR,
          Marcia, we continue this discussion
          in my office.

They move to an office down the hall.

INT.JEFFREY'S OFFICE-DAY

They sit down and Marcia closes the door.

                         JEFFREY
              I didn't want to have this
              conversation in front of the others
              but the truth is, JR, we can't
              really afford to pay you a salary
              if you can't or won't bring in some
              fee work of your own. You can't
              just do the pro bono stuff from now
              on.

                         MARCIA
              You could be making more than the
              paralegal wages we are paying you
              now if you would take some of these
              defense files. Don't you want to
              make more money?

                         JR
              Are you giving me some kind of
              ultimatum?

                         MARCIA
              We've been carrying you for quite
              awhile now because we love your
              work. If you could find a way to
              get paid for all these housing
              cases I'd say go for it. But we all
              know there is no money there.

                         JR
              What if I got a grant? There are so
              many of these files, we have to do
              something.

                         JEFFREY
              If that's what you want to do, then
              we need to look for someone who can
              work these new cases.

JR is taken aback.

                         MARCIA
              You need to give this some serious
              thought, JR. We have to cut your
              pay until you figure out how you
              can generate some fees for this
              work you want to do.

INT.JR'S APARTMENT-DAY

JR slams down an armload of files and pours herself a drink.

                    SANDY
Before you get settled in, you
should know we just got a big rent
increase posted on the door today.

                    JR
What?? Did everyone get one?

                    SANDY
Apparently. So, an extra $200 a
month, how are we going to do this?

                    JR
That's just great. They want to cut
my pay too.

                    SANDY
WHY!!

                    JR
They want me to do more claims
work, say they may bring in
somebody else if I don't cut back
on the clinic work.

                    SANDY
          (agitated)
And you don't want to do boring
legal work for real money when you
can do welfare work for free?

                    JR
There's a crisis out there, Sandy.
These sick guys are getting evicted
because of the panic.

                    SANDY
          (more agitated)
JR you can't save everybody! WE'RE
going to be evicted if you can't
make any more money. Why do you
have to be so stubborn? Why do you
have to put the whole world first
when we could be even a little more
comfortable. I can't deal with this
anymore. I'm not going to work my
ass off to bring in more money when
you don't even care about OUR life.

                    JR
I'll talk to the manager about the
rent. And what do you mean I don't
care about our life?

                    SANDY
          OUR life, JR, not your fabulous
          superhero career. What about US?

                    JR
          My work is important, it's making a
          difference.

                    SANDY
                   (screaming)
          It's stubborn and selfish. What are
          you trying to prove anyway?

                    JR
                   (calmly)
          I want to open my own clinic and
          need you to stand behind me.

                    SANDY
          Have you not heard a word I said??

                    JR
          Sandy....

Sandy grabs a jacket and heads out the door, slamming it as
she leaves. Exasperated, JR tops off her glass.

EXT.MISSION LEGAL CLINIC-DAY

A for sale sign is in the window. JR stops to look at the
facade of the building and opens the door smiling.

INT.MISSION LEGAL CLINIC-DAY

Raymond is in his office. JR stands at his door.

                    JR
          So the building is for sale?

                    RAYMOND
          Yep. I need to move on. I can't
          carry the building and the practice
          too. The funding for poverty law
          services is drying up and I am just
          burned out.

                    JR
          Is your board going to bring in
          another attorney?

                         RAYMOND
          The board is me, my mom and my
          uncle and he has dementia. If we
          can sell the building, I'm closing
          the practice.

                         JR
          Can I make a phone call?

JR closes the door to the conference room and picks up the
phone. She is visible through the large glass window.

INT.DAD'S PLUSH OFFICE-DAY

A receptionist picks up the phone and nods. She patches the
call into Dad's office and we see him pick up his phone. A
colleague that he was speaking with stands and leaves. After
a smiling greeting, Dad is listening and shaking his head.
Then he listens longer, asks a few questions, hesitates and
then nods affirmatively.

INT.MISSION LEGAL CLINIC-DAY

JR reappears at Raymond's office door.

                         JR
          Raymond, I want to buy the building
          and the practice from you. Let's
          talk.

                         RAYMOND
          Are you sure you want to do this?
          There's an apartment upstairs too.

                         JR
          Perfect.

They shake hands.

INT.JR'S APARTMENT-DAY

JR bursts through the door.

                         JR
          Hey Sandy guess what!

Half the furniture is gone, Sandy has moved out. JR throws
her briefcase and kicks at a pile of books on the floor.

                         JR (CONT'D)
          SANDY!

JR walks through the half empty apartment. Her anger melts briefly into sadness when she sees a picture of the two of them still on the fridge. Then it hardens into anger again.

INT.JR'S OFFICE-DAY

JR is packing as is Rose, the receptionist. The new attorney is working in the conference room. Everyone hugs her goodbye. Marcia follows her out the door.

>   MARCIA
>   Don't be a stranger, call me up if
>   you change your mind. The least you
>   could have done is not take our
>   best receptionist with you.

>   JR
>   That was her idea. Thanks for
>   everything.

They hug and exchange a look of respect and affection. Jeffrey avoids eye contact as she leaves.

INT.MISSION LEGAL CLINIC-DAY

A van is parked in front of the clinic with lettering on the side reading FRINGE ELECTRIC. JR comes in as Cat is hanging a new sign in the front window which reads "Mission Legal Clinic, JR Bensen Attorney at Law". Rose hands her several notes. There are people waiting to see her. She goes into her office and starts leafing through the notes, takes out her notepad and picks up the phone. We see her talking on the phone. Time passes with people coming and going through her office, both staff and clients. Cat, wearing a tool belt and moving a step ladder, is hanging light fixtures in JR's office when Rose taps on the door.

>   ROSE
>   Ok if I close up and get out of
>   here before someone else comes in?

JR notices that Cat and Rose are eyeing each other with interest.

>   JR
>   Of course. I'll go through all this
>   and make some notes. Are you in
>   tomorrow?

                    ROSE
          Yes, and I can probably get a
          couple of interns to come in on
          Thursday afternoon for a few hours
          if you need them.

                    JR
          Great. So, have you two met? Rose,
          this is my homegirl Cat.

Cat and Rose exchange a smile and leave the office together.
JR looks out the window and sees them chatting next to Cat's
FRINGE ELECTRIC van. JR smiles, amused. She looks around the
cluttered office with the piles of case files with a sigh of
satisfaction. Then she reaches into her desk and pours a
shot of bourbon into a coffee cup.

INT.SAN FRANCISCO GENERAL HOSPITAL-DAY

JR walks past the hospital sign and in through the doors of
the old building, gets into an elevator to the 6th floor,
exits and walks down the hall to Ward 86.

She checks in at the nursing station where she is directed to
a room halfway down the hall. JR taps on the open door and
enters. JOSH, a very ill young man is in the bed. DAVID, his
less sick partner is sitting next to him.

                    JR
          Hi. Are you JOSH and DAVID?

                    DAVID
          That's us.

                    JR
          JR Bensen, Mission Legal Clinic.
          How are you guys doing?

                    DAVID
          Not so good. We got an eviction
          notice yesterday. I just got him
          in here in the morning and came
          home to find this notice on the
          door. Our rent is paid up and
          everything. Can they just kick us
          out like that?

                    JR
          This doesn't specify why, just be
          out in 5 days. Do you know why you
          are being evicted?

                    DAVID
          The manager saw us leave in an
          ambulance so we figure he knows
          about this. I'm feeling pretty good
          and so far I can still bring in a
          paycheck, but I can't take care of
          him, work and look for another
          place for us to live.

                    JOSH
          Our neighbor, Michael, got kicked
          out last week. He's got karposi's
          with all these awful lesions. His
          brother came and got him. He was
          really sick.

                    JR
          Sounds like your landlord doesn't
          like gay people.

                    DAVID
          Not sick ones for sure. I don't
          know what we are going to do.

                    JR
          I will contact him with some strong
          language advising him he has to
          properly file and serve notice and
          show good cause. I can't guarantee
          you'll be able to stay long but it
          will buy you some time. If he's
          kicked others out the same way
          there may be more I can do.

                    DAVID
          We'd be grateful for any extension
          we can get. I just don't want to
          come home and find the locks
          changed and our stuff sitting in
          the driveway.

INT.WARD 86-DAY

JR is talking to Josh and David through the doorway as a
group of nurses walk by. In the middle of the group is Skye,
older and in uniform, her hair tied back. She does not see
JR.

The group moves down the hall and into a larger room where
the nurses take their seats.

JR is back in the hall and passes the nurses' classroom
without glancing inside. Neither JR or Skye see each other.

INT.NURSES' CLASSROOM-DAY

JR has just walked by in the hall.

> HEAD NURSE
> That's pretty much how this new
> AIDS ward works. I know a couple of
> you, Skye and Jean, are new to
> nursing. Congratulations on passing
> your exams. This is a tough place
> to start your careers but these
> patients need our service and
> compassion just like all patients
> do. Check your schedule. You'll be
> shadowing another nurse and
> rotating through all the stations
> for awhile. See you tomorrow.

Skye and the other nurses make their way out of the building.

INT.BUS STOP-DAY

A bus pulls up to where Skye and another nurse are standing
and she gets on. When the bus doors open again she gets off
in front of Arlo's Haight victorian. She goes up the steps.

INT.ARLO'S ROOM-DAY

Arlo is in bed, very ill, looking out the window. Skye
enters.

> SKYE
> Hey there boyfriend. How do you
> feel today?

> ARLO
> Exhausted and scared. How was your
> first day on the job?

> SKYE
> It's going to be hard but I can do
> this. It is such a relief to know I
> will have a decent steady income
> for the first time ever.

> ARLO
> I'm proud of you, Skye. You'll make
> a great nurse. How are things at
> home with... what's his name.....?

                    SKYE
          Yeah, HIM. I think I hate him. I
          want out. He has no respect for me
          or what I can do. Just because he
          has all this money he figures he
          can do whatever he wants. He
          humored me by letting me go to
          school as long as I was there when
          he got home. I'm leaving him as
          soon as I get my first paycheck.

                    ARLO
          You know you can always stay here.

                    SKYE
          I know but I need to have my own
          place. I have never in my life had
          a place that I'm not sharing with
          anyone. But I'll be here to take
          care of you. You know that, right?

                    ARLO
          I want that for you, a place of
          your very own. Are you still in
          touch with that cab driver friend
          of yours?

                    SKYE
          JR? No, I haven't looked her up
          since I came here. I'm sure she's a
          big time lawyer by now and probably
          has a beautiful girlfriend.

                    ARLO
          You don't know that. So I take it
          she doesn't know you are here.

Skye shakes her head no.

EXT.BUS STOP-NIGHT

Skye leaves to catch another bus, this time getting off in
front of a swanky apartment building where she is greeted by
a doorman as she enters.

AIDS HEADLINES MONTAGE:

RARE CANCER FOUND IN HOMOSEXUALS

AIDS THE BUBONIC PLAGUE OF THE 21ST CENTURY?

SURGE IN HIV INFECTIONS AMOUNG GAYS AND BISEXUALS

AIDS RELATED EVICTIONS ON THE RISE IN SAN FRANCISCO.

INT.WARD 86-DAY

Josh has died. JR comforts David. The halls are lined with
sick young men. JR speaks to several of them as she walks
down the halls.

In one room she finds Cameron, who is very thin, his hair is
falling out. EUNICE, his sister is at his bedside.

> JR
> Hey there, Camomile. They treating
> you ok?

> CAMERON
> (weakly)
> JR! You remember Eunice?

> JR
> Yes, of course. How are things in
> Long Beach?

> EUNICE
> Oh things are good as they can be.
> We're clearing out his old room to
> bring him home tomorrow.

> CAMERON
> Hey JR, remember how we sang all
> the way to San Francisco when we
> moved up here?

> JR
> That was a great trip. You kept
> shoplifting snacks at every gas
> station we stopped at.

> CAMERON
> It was a great ride, my friend.

Cameron reaches for JR's hand which JR takes with an
affectionate squeeze.

> JR
> That it was.

Cameron starts coughing violently. Eunice waves for a nurse
from the door and several staff rush in. JR backs away from
the bed, holding Cameron's hand until it's beyond their
reach, and then reluctantly releasing it. She retreats and
watches from the doorway.

                    EUNICE
        We need to keep him quiet for now.
        I'll keep you posted.

JR and Cameron manage a wave before the door is closed and JR
is left in the hall facing the closed door. Her head drops,
she catches a deep breath to steady herself, bites her lip,
lingers a few moments then turns and heads for the elevator
without making eye contact with anyone else.

INT.JR'S OFFICE-DAY

The scene with Rose leaving the office is repeated. This
time, JR is staring out the window barely responding to say
good night. When Rose opens the office the next morning, JR
is asleep on the office couch wearing the same clothes.

EXT.JR'S OFFICE-DAY

JR'S motorcycle is parked on the sidewalk by the entrance of
the office.

EXT.NAMES PROJECT STOREFRONT-DAY

It is a cold and foggy day. The signage reads The Names
Project. Cosmic Lady is looking at the panels hanging in the
window. JR, subdued, is walking up the street and doesn't
notice her.

INT.NAMES PROJECT STOREFRONT-DAY

Skye and several other people are working at sewing machines.
Skye brings a panel and hangs it in the front window. It has
Arlo's picture on it.

EXT.NAMES PROJECT STOREFRONT-DAY

Just as Skye turns away, JR is walking by. They don't see
each other. JR stops in her tracks and backs up when she sees
the panel in the window and recognizes Arlo. A moment passes
as she looks at the panels in the window.

                    COSMIC LADY
        Our blessed children are dying.

JR turns quickly away dazed and catches her breath, and walks
slowly away. Cosmic Lady can be seen over JR's shoulder
looking at her.

                    COSMIC LADY (CONT'D)
                  (loud enough for JR to
                   hear)
          Save yourself.

JR stops briefly, and blinks hard then continues walking.
Cosmic Lady turns to the window again.

INT.NAMES PROJECT STOREFRONT-DAY

Skye looks over the shoulder of a young man working at a
sewing machine. Cosmic Lady is visible in the window as she
turns back to look inside.

INT.MISSION LEGAL CLINIC-DAY

Rose calls JR on the phone upstairs.

                    ROSE
          JR, I thought you had an appearance
          today. Opposing counsel just
          called. Your client was able to
          persuade the judge to continue the
          hearing instead of dismissing it.

                    JR (O.S.)
          Oh crap. I must have overslept.
          What time is it?

                    ROSE
          Almost 10.

                    JR (O.S.)
          Shit. I'll be down in a few
          minutes.

JR enters the office more than a little disheveled. Two law
clerks look up then look away. Clients are waiting. JR stops
to look through the mail, opening one of the letters hastily.
Obviously it is bad news. JR looks over to a Latina with a
baby and young African American man in the waiting area.

                    JR (CONT'D)
          I'm very sorry, I won't be able to
          talk to you today but I will look
          over what you filled out with Rose
          here and call you. Thank you for
          coming in.

They leave and JR turns to Rose and the law clerks. Rose is
holding a black poster with a pink triangle and the caption
Silence=Death ACTUP San Francisco.

                    ROSE
          ACT UP wants to know if they can
          hang a poster in your window and
          maybe talk to you about using the
          conference room for a meeting.

                    JR
              (dazed and not making eye
               contact)
          Sure. It looks like a light day
          today, why don't you take off. I
          need to unplug the phone and get
          caught up on some stuff, maybe
          close the office for awhile. I'll
          let you know what's happening in a
          few days.

                    ROSE
          What's going on, is everything ok?

                    JR
              (looking away)
          Just go please, Rose.

JR is looking out the window when Rose and the others leave.
When the door closes, the roaring in her head begins. She
slides into a chair before losing her balance, head in her
hands.

INT.UPSCALE NEIGHBORHOOD BAR-NIGHT

JR is sitting alone at the bar staring into her drink. Later
her head is cradled in her arms on the bar when Marcia taps
her on the shoulder.

                    JR
          Marcia, what are you doing here?

                    MARCIA
          Your friendly bartender called me
          instead of putting you in a cab.
          Are you ok? We're a little worried
          about you and your friend there.

                    JR
              (quite drunk, holding up
               the glass affectionately)
          My lil friend here has been in my
          family for generations. Hard to say
          goodbye to an ol' friend. My grant
          was denied, don't know how I'm
          going to keep the clinic open.

                    MARCIA
          I know. Raymond told me. You did
          great keeping it open as long as
          you did. You know you can come back
          and work with us if you want.
          C'mon, let's go home.

EXT.MISSION LEGAL CLINIC-NIGHT

A cab pulls up, JR and Marcia get out. JR looks at the
signage reading Mission Legal Clinic. The lights are still on
in the empty office. The motorcycle is parked by the door.

                    JR
          I'm ok. You don't have to tuck me
          in.

                    MARCIA
          Get some rest. Let's talk in the
          morning.

JR stands at the outside door to the apartment as Marcia gets
back in the cab and leaves. JR watches the cab drive away in
the reflection of the window. When the cab is out of sight,
JR looks down the street and then looks at the motorcycle.

INT.MARCIA'S CAB-NIGHT

The cab pulls away and starts down the street. A block away
it is stopped at a light when JR blows past them on the
motorcycle.

                    MARCIA
          Oh no. Follow that bike.

Marcia's cab follows JR through the light traffic onto a
windy side street. They catch up just in time to see JR miss
a turn, drop the bike and slide into some trees.

Moments later an ambulance races by with lights flashing.

INT.HOSPITAL ER-NIGHT

JR is bandaged up with one arm in a cast and there are dark
contusions on the side of her face. IVs and monitors are
attached. She comes to with a nurse and doctor attending to
her.

                    DOCTOR
          Well look who joined us. How do you
          feel?

                        JR
          Ouch.

                        DOCTOR
          Try not to move too much, we just
          got that arm set. By the way your
          blood alcohol level was .18. You
          are lucky to have survived that.

                        JR
               (trying to sit up)
          I didn't hurt anyone else, did I.

                        DOCTOR
          The paramedic said you tried to
          cuff him when they strapped you to
          the gurney but he'll be ok. You
          have a couple of friends here.

Rose and Marcia come in.

                        ROSE
          Hey boss. Look at you, joyriding
          after hours.

                        JR
          I know. Who do I think I am?

                        ROSE
          You are JR Bensen, uncompromising
          defender of justice and
          professional shit disturber.

                        JR
          I'm not so sure about that. I
          couldn't save them. I can't do this
          anymore. I have to close the
          clinic.

                        ROSE
          I know.

1998.

The painted ladies Victorians on Alamo Square and a shot of
Dolores Park with people lounging in the sun. Dogs are
running freely.

EXT.MISSION LEGAL CLINIC-DAY

Faded paint on the legal services sign. A newer sign reading
JR Bensen Investigations is now in the window.

The ACT UP San Francisco poster is still there along with a large rainbow flag. JR, back to being a cab driver, gets out of a newer model cab parked at the curb. She's older and fuller and looking very working class butch.

The door of the clinic is open and as she goes in the sign by the door shows the AA logo. When the door reopens a while later, Lucy as a stylishly dressed 20ish Latina emerges.

Her younger brother Roman, tattooed and in street gangster dress follows her out along with a number of others including several mainstream looking people, a leather gay man, a couple of queens and a drag king dressed as Elvis. JR is one of the last to emerge.

                    JR
          Elvis, glad you could make it.

                    ELVIS
          Good to see you again, brother.

They hug. Lucy and Roman approach JR.

                    LUCY
          He told me about you being here. I
          wanted to see you. You probably
          don't remember us but you helped
          our mother get a restraining order
          against our father.

                    JR
          I thought you looked familiar, how
          old were you then.

                    ROMAN
          I was 5 and she was 7. Our mom was
          Carmen Ramirez.

                    JR
             (reaching out and hugging
              both of them together)
          Lucy and Roman, my god, I am so
          sorry about your mother. I always
          wondered whatever happened to you.

                    ROMAN
          Don't be sorry. It's not your
          fault. You saved us.

                    LUCY
          Mom was able to hide us, just like
          you told her. You gave her hope
          just long enough to get us to a
          safe place.
             (MORE)

                        LUCY (CONT'D)
          So we wanted to tell you that. You
          helped a lot of women at that
          shelter.

                        JR
          I did what I could. What are you
          guys doing now?

                        ROMAN
          I got my own struggles but I know I
          will never be like him. She's
          taking cop classes at City College.

                        JR
          No kidding!

                        LUCY
          It's hard but I'm sticking with it.
          I'm trying to get him into it too.
          We should know enough about police
          work to fit right in.

                        JR
          Proud of you two. If you need
          anything, you can find me here.

They linger a moment on the sidewalk before JR gets back into
her cab.

INT.JR'S CAB-DAY

A gay couple and a lesbian couple pile into the cab. They are
very happy.

                        JR
          Where to?

                        GAY MAN
          To Julius' Castle!

                        LESBIAN
          We're on our honeymoon!

                        PASSENGERS IN UNISON
          WE JUST GOT MARRIED!!

JR laughs a big joyful laugh.

EXT.FINANCIAL DISTRICT CAB STAND-DAY

JR dials on her cell phone.

INT.HOSPITAL ROOM-DAY

Dad is resting when his phone rings.

> JR (O.S.)
> Hey Dad. It's Jackie.

> DAD
> Hi Jackie.

INT.JR'S CAB-DAY

> JR
> How are you feeling? Mark said you
> collapsed and they aren't sure what
> happened.

> DAD (O.S.)
> Yeah, I got really dizzy, feeling
> better now. I think they are going
> to run a few more tests.

> JR
> You sound real tired. Hey, I'm
> driving down in the next day or so.

> DAD (O.S.)
> I should be going home later today.
> You can stay at the condo. How's
> things with you? Still doing
> investigations?

> JR
> Yeah, finishing up a big case so
> I'm taking some time off. Turning
> in a report to the DA's office
> nailing one our more infamous
> slumlords.

> DAD (O.S.)
> Still the troublemaker. Bring a
> girlfriend if you want.

> JR
> Don't have one. I can't seem to
> figure that relationship stuff out.
> Kinda used to being on my own.

> DAD (O.S.)
> Your mom and I didn't exactly set a
> good example did we?

                         JR
          Not sure I'd agree with that.

                         DAD (O.S.)
          You've always done it your own way,
          kiddo. Well, Mark's here and wants
          to talk to you. So we'll see you in
          a couple of days?

                         JR
          I'll be down there Thursday or
          Friday. I just need to wrap up a
          couple of things here.

INT.HOSPITAL ROOM-DAY

Mark enters and takes the phone.

                         MARK
          Hey there.

                         JR (O.S.)
          So what's going on with him?

                         MARK
          Right now he seems to be thinking
          clearly but lately he's not been
          himself. Getting lost, wandering
          around in the street in his
          pajamas. Things like that. Not
          knowing his name.

                         JR (O.S)
          Ok. I'll be down there in a couple
          days and just plan on staying with
          him for awhile.

                         MARK
          Lucky you got to talk to him when
          he was clear enough to know who
          are. He didn't recognize me just a
          few hours ago.

INT.JR'S CAB-DAY

                         JR
          How are Barbara and the kids?

                         MARK (O.S.)
          We're ok, things are kind of
          ...upsetting. Sonja wants to be
          called Sonny and... it's been hard.

                              JR
                    Could be worse. She could be a
                    drunk or a heroin addict... or a
                    divorce lawyer.

                         MARK (O.S.)
                    Funny.

JR is watching the door of the office building in front of
her. She looks at her watch.

                              JR
                    Gotta go, we'll talk later.

EXT.FINANCIAL DISTRICT CAB STAND-DAY

JR's cab is between two other cabs in line. She is checking
her watch as she watches the door. The front cab pulls away.
As JR waits, Skye, comes out of another building and walks
toward JR's cab. Her hippie look is long gone and she has a
strong, mature, confident bearing. Just as she reaches for
the door, JR spots a man in a business suit coming out of the
building just ahead. She jumps out of the cab and rushes up
behind him, intentionally slamming into him and making him
drop his briefcase.

                         BUSINESS MAN
                    What the hell is wrong with you?

                              JR
                    So sorry, Mr Clark.

She picks up her briefcase and holds it just out his reach.

                         JR (CONT'D)
                    Willard Clark, right?

                         BUSINESS MAN
                    Yes. How did you know my name?

                              JR
                    Good morning, sir. You have been
                    served. Have a great day.

JR hands him a paper with the briefcase. JR turns and walks
away smirking as the man looks at the documents and then
curses.

INT.SKYE'S CAB-DAY

The next cab pulls away from the curb with Skye in it. JR
and Skye do not see each other.

                        DRIVER
            Where to, ma'am?

                        SKYE
            SFO. The guy ahead of you just
            missed a good fare.

                        DRIVER
            Oh, that's ok. She just served that
            dude with papers he for sure did
            not want to see. She be like the
            process server to the stars or
            somethin. She can find anybody.
            She'll knock um down, trip um,
            whatever. One time she was way up
            in one of these big office
            buildings and she followed some
            dude into the mens room. He be
            standin there with his business in
            his hands and she just puts the
            papers in his coat pocket and tells
            him have a good day and walks out.
            I wisht I coulda seen that dude's
            face.

                        SKYE
            She? Really?

She turns to look at the cab driver/process server but JR's
back is turned and she doesn't get a good look.

                        DRIVER
            So where you flyin out to?

                        SKYE
            Long Beach. Back to visit my kids
            and grandkids.

                        DRIVER
            When I go home, I always like to
            check out the ol' stompin grounds
            to see how things have changed.
            Brings back memories.

                        SKYE
            If they exist after all these
            years.

                        DRIVER
            Got that right.

INT.JR'S CAR-DAY

JR is on the freeway, listening to music. Daylight shifts to
twilight, her phone rings. She puts it on speakerphone.

> JR
> Mark, what's up. I'm on my way,
> should be there in about 4 hours.

> MARK (O.S.)
> Jackie. Dad's gone. The nurse went
> to check on him and he was just...
> gone. I was just on my way back
> from getting a bite to eat.

JR pulls off the road and puts her hands over her face. Then
she calmly takes a deep breath and stares off into the
darkness.

> JR
> (whispering)
> Dad.

EXT.GRAVESIDE-DAY

Another funeral. Everyone is a generation older than at
Grandma's funeral. JR and Mark and his family are in the
front row. His kids are dressed in more street grunge style
with Sonja/Sonny in boys clothes, sporting a light mustache.
Surfer Dave and his teenagers are in the row behind, 3 boys
and a girl. His kids are clean cut and dressed very
conservatively.

FREEZE FRAME and SHUTTER CLICKS

INT.UPSCALE SUBURBAN HOME-DAY

JR and Mark are in a reception line. Aunt Rae is in a
wheelchair being assisted by a nurse. She scowls at JR as she
is wheeled past. JR acknowledges her with a nod and a smile.
The line ends, Mark moves to the bar and JR to the food.
Surfer Dave approaches with his kids. He is tan, slightly
balding and a little portly, dressed in a Hawaiian shirt
under a suit jacket.

> SURFER DAVE
> Hey you guys, you remember my
> cousin, Jackie? She was a real
> pitbull lawyer in San Francisco and
> took on the whole police department
> in a riot. Hey, you still got your
> Harley?

                    JR
          Got rid of it a few years ago. Ok,
          see if I got this right, you are
          Tyler, Scottie, Robin and James. I
          haven't seen you guys in a long
          time and you know you've changed so
          I won't say how little you were
          then.

Surfer Dave and Tyler move away.

                    ROBIN
          Were you really in a riot?

                    JR
          It was just a demonstration that
          got out of hand.

                    SCOTTIE
          We read about it in school and I
          did a report on the White Night
          Riot. It was cool to show that
          picture of you from the newspaper.

                    JR
          Really? They actually taught
          something about the gay rights
          movement in school?

                    JAMES
          It was modern social history and
          the civil rights movement and
          feminist stuff.

Barbara, glass of wine in hand, approaches when JR is alone.
Barbara, looking more matronly these days, approaches JR.
She has clearly had more than one glass of wine.

                    JR
          Barbara.

                    BARBARA
          Jackie.

                    JR
          Your kids are all grown up now too.

                    BARBARA
          Well, yes, they are but it seems we
          have a long way to go. Peter wants
          to drop out of college. Brenda is
          crazy about a man 30 years older
          than she is and Sonja...Sonny is in
          a world of her own...his own.

                    JR
          They find their own path. They are
          all ok.

                    BARBARA
                (amusing herself)
          Brenda actually said to me the
          other day that I should be like
          Aunt Jackie and quit drinking.

Mark, with cocktail in hand, is talking loudly with a couple
of other guests at the bar.

                    BARBARA (CONT'D)
          I used to hate you but the kids
          think you're cool.

                    JR
          I pretty much didn't like you
          either. Good thing we outgrew that,
          huh?

                    BARBARA
          I think we've outgrown that. Your
          Dad always stuck up for you. Mark
          could never figure that out. But
          then you never sucked up to him
          like everyone else in the family
          did. I think that was it.

                    JR
          He was a good man in his own
          controlling, overbearing,
          borderline abusive way. It was all
          about the family with him.

                    BARBARA
          I'll miss him.

                    JR
          Me too. Where's Sonny?

                    BARBARA
          That's her...him over there by the
          window looking like she.. he..

                    JR
          ...they..

                    BARBARA
          ..they would like to fly away.

JR approaches Sonny and they chat. Sonny is clearly in
transition. Old school butch meets millennial transman.

Their conversation ends with a bro hug and a fist bump. JR
moves back into the main part of the room.

Surfer Dave approaches.

>   JR
>   Look at you all respectable. Your
>   kids look great.

>   SURFER DAVE
>   They are cool kids. 'Course they
>   live with their mom most of the
>   time but they are all right. Love
>   school and everything. James wants
>   to be a friggin accountant. But I
>   get um out on the boat when I can
>   and it's great. They work in the
>   restaurant with me too.

>   JR
>   You have a restaurant?

>   SURFER DAVE
>   Got three! Dave's Burger Shack.
>   Opening Number four in Manhattan
>   Beach in a couple of weeks.

>   JR
>   No kidding! You turned into your
>   Dad after all.

>   SURFER DAVE
>   (laughing)
>   Oh, I wouldn't go that far!

More guests mingle and soon the last of the group leaves.

INT.DAD'S CONDO-NIGHT

JR lets herself in and stands in the hallway taking in all
the family photos on the wall. There she sees them as a young
family. Jackie and Mark as 6 and 10 year olds. They are all
smiling except Jackie who is wearing a frilly dress. It
brings a smile to her face.

>   JR
>   Poor kid.

JR settles in at the table with her laptop.

FACEBOOK SCREENSHOT

A friend request from Skye. JR shakes her head in disbelief
and answers 'confirm'.

EXT.STREET-DAY

JR drives slowly past the renovated Ripples bar and smiles. A
few more turns and she cruises past the brown house which has
been restored to its architectural grandeur.

INT.EGG HEAVEN CAFE-DAY

The Egg Heaven coffee shop looks exactly the same. The bikini
poster is gone, replaced by a photo of Ralph and a sign IN
MEMORIAM. JR sits at a booth with her back to the door,
orders and opens her laptop. Behind her, Skye enters the cafe
and sits at a table by the window and opens her laptop.
Their backs are to each other.

FACEBOOK SCREENSHOT

A message from Skye comes up on JR's screen. JR is typing her
replies.

SKYE: Good to finally connect with you. It's been a long
time. I'm surprised you even remember me.

JR: Of course, I remember you. I've often wondered whatever
happened to you. What are you doing these days?

Skye: Just retired from nursing. Are you still practicing
law?

JR: Nursing? I had no idea. Nope, gave up practicing law. I
run an investigations business now. A lot less stressful. How
are your kids?

Skye: Grown up and married, and I've got 4 grandkids. They
all live in Long Beach. Are you still in San Francisco?

JR: My office is. Right now I'm in Long Beach for my dad's
funeral yesterday.

Skye: Sorry about your dad.

JR: Thanks. I drove by your old house today. Somebody really
fixed it up. Having breakfast at the Egg Heaven right now for
old time sake.

Skye looks quickly around the restaurant and sees JR at the
booth nearby. In shock.

Skye: I'm in Long Beach right now too.

JR: Really?? Where??

Skye: Look behind you.

JR turns and sees Skye at the table by the window. They both stand and walk toward each other.

Montage of News Footage

San Francisco Dyke March Banner with the huge crowd behind it.

The Marriage Equality Demonstrations

The 2017 Womens March on Washington

FADE OUT

(CONT'D)

Made in the USA
Coppell, TX
23 November 2019